I AM ARIEL SHARON

I AM ARIEL SHARON

A NOVEL

YARA EL-GHADBAN

TRANSLATED BY WAYNE GRADY

ARACHNIDE

First published as *Je suis Ariel Sharon* in 2018 by Mémoire d'encrier
First published in English in 2020 by House of Anansi Press Inc.
www.houseofanansi.com

24 23 22 21 20   1 2 3 4 5

Library and Archives Canada Cataloguing in Publication

Title: I Am Ariel Sharon / Yara El-Ghadban ; translated by Wayne Grady.
Other titles: Je suis Ariel Sharon. English
Names: El-Ghadban, Yara, 1976– author.
Description: Translation of: Je suis Ariel Sharon.
Identifiers: Canadiana (print) 2020020842X | Canadiana (ebook) 20200208438 |
ISBN 9781487007973 (softcover) | ISBN 9781487007980 (EPUB) |
ISBN 9781487007997 (Kindle)
Subjects: LCSH: Sharon, Ariel—Fiction.
Classification: LCC PS8609.E334 J413 2020 | DDC C843/.6—dc23

Cover design: Etienne Bienvenu

Canada Council Conseil des Arts
for the Arts   du Canada

ONTARIO ARTS COUNCIL
CONSEIL DES ARTS DE L'ONTARIO
an Ontario government agency
un organisme du gouvernement de l'Ontario

*We acknowledge the financial support of the Government of Canada through the
National Translation Program for Book Publishing, an initiative of the* Action Plan
for Official Languages—2018–2023: Investing in Our Future, *for our translation
activities.*

Printed and bound in Canada

To those whom History
has prevented from being ordinary.

This is not a biography, but fiction. Only fiction can work within History's flaws. And only the novel makes our meeting possible.

Y.E.

January 2, 2018

Ah Rita
Between us a million birds and images
Of innumerable trysts
Riddled with bullets.

Mahmoud Darwish

I AM ARIEL SHARON

TEL AVIV, JANUARY 4, 2006
POLITICAL UPHEAVAL IN ISRAEL
PRIME MINISTER ARIEL SHARON FLOORED BY A STROKE

Arik...

ARIK, THE LION, PLUNGED INTO A COMA
A FEW MONTHS PRIOR TO THE ELECTIONS

Arik...

THE FORMER STRONGMAN OF ISRAEL IS BEING
KEPT ALIVE IN THE TEL HASHOMER SHEBA HOSPITAL
OUTSIDE OF TEL AVIV

Arik...

THE POWERS OF THE MAN KNOWN AS THE
GRANDFATHER OF THE NATION TRANSFERRED TO
HIS DEPUTY PRIME MINISTER, EHUD OLMERT

Arik...

KADIMA, THE CENTRIST PARTY FOUNDED BY
ARIEL SHARON SHORTLY BEFORE HIS COLLAPSE,
WINS A SLIM MAJORITY

Arik...

Arik...

Arik! Follow my voice. Don't look for the light. Don't look for your body. Arik! Yes, it's you I'm talking to. Are you cold? You're shivering. Patience, have patience. You'll feel better soon. I'm here. I'll explain everything. Don't try to speak. I'll be your mouth, your eyes, your body.

You're floating. In liquid. It's the caress of the void. Immerse yourself in it. Let yourself be swallowed up in its warmth. You'll not suffocate. On the contrary, you'll breathe more easily and hear better, too. Who knows? You might gradually recover your sight, even your speech. So, don't seek yourself out. You no longer exist. You are dying, Arik. Slowly.

Be calm, be calm. Here is truth. The truth doesn't hurt. It doesn't judge. You are losing your faculties, your sense of things. Who you are, your age, your face. None of it matters. I am everything you no longer are. Your loves, your hatreds, your dreams, your fears, your

4

regrets. I hear the words, the doubts, the terrors. I see the child, the man, his rise, his fall.

I know the precise moment of your demise. For days and days, clichés pour in from all sides:

Ariel Sharon, the charismatic commander, surrounded by swirling eddies of sand in the middle of the desert. You giving orders. You plotting the positions of Egyptian troops on a map.

Ariel Sharon, sitting around the table of a community centre, sharing a meal with settlers. Lily, your beloved, at your side. You laugh heartily between bites.

Ariel Sharon, your head barely visible among the bodyguards protecting you from the faithful at the Al-Aqsa Mosque in Jerusalem's Old City.

Ariel Sharon in the Knesset, an accusatory finger pointing at a member of the Opposition.

The more the years pass, the more weight you gain. Your obesity takes on the grotesque dimensions of a glutton whose entire body has become a mouth. Your stomach swings on its own whenever you stand up or take a step. Suddenly this is all you are, sagging pounds of flesh drooping over your buried belt. And what it has devoured, this flesh! Faces, voices, stories, places, time, territory, houses, futures, hopes, shrieks, dreams, nightmares, legs crawling on the ground and hands reaching up to the sky. They stir beneath your skin, these desires, hungers, furies wolfed down quickly, so quickly, before there's even time to chew on them. Their churning creates hollows and lumps, deforming your stomach. And suddenly, here you are: Ariel Sharon, in the abyss of your body.

An entire life unravels behind the dispassionate voice of the journalist delivering the news:

Tel Aviv, January 4, 2006. Prime Minister Ariel Sharon has lapsed into a deep coma. The stroke has occurred two months before the general election that, according to polls, will return him to power at the head of Kadima, the centrist party he recently founded.

I smile.

Don't give me a hard time for smiling, I can't help it. I carry my story and those of so many other women, Arik. And though, like you, their bodies may elude them, they've not lost their memories.

I hear their voices as I do your own. The one you hide in the soundproofed room that is your soul.

I am the fire that burns within.

I am love, I am melancholy.

I am silence.

Silence...

Truths, hushed.

Confessions, stifled.

Agonies, dragging themselves across the floor.

I am the cry!

The disgust. The bitterness.

The satisfaction at the news of your stroke.

There you go. He got what he deserved!

A fate more awful than death: a half-death, or worse. A half-life.

Arik, are you listening? Do my words give you the chills? Don't run away. Wrap yourself in my voice. The roughest cloth is also the warmest, as you well know, you who sat up all night long in your father's fields in a coarse woollen coat.

Let me come near, caress your eyelids, put my own eyes behind them. Now do you see, Arik? The necks, chins, chests, arms of the doctors, paramedics, and nurses bending over you? They're pushing your bed into the operating room.

Float, Arik. Savour the lightness of death.

You're not a believer, but still you say a little prayer before the plane takes off. Out of superstition, maybe habit. You believe in the Last Judgement no more than you do in morality. Neither do I. Does that surprise you, coming from an angel? You're an atheist, and yet you think me an angel. No, Arik. Angels don't consider the question of whether or not they're on the side of good or evil. They're not born, they don't die. They just are. There's no more to it than that.

As for me, I was young once, beautiful, and in love with a boy who had the gift of words. He used to tell me the divine lived in my eyes. He was a poet and I was his poem. He wrote me so that I wouldn't grow up, so I'd remain the little Jewish girl with golden tresses, whose cheeks he liked to pinch. But he was the one who didn't grow up. And despite his poems, my hair lost its glow.

Say my name, Arik. All the wretched of this land sing my poem.

No, I'm not an angel. Injustice roars in me, has its hands around my neck, plants my feet firmly on the ground. My wings flap uselessly in the air. They beat the wind beneath my arms. The wind blows and blows against my arms until it breaks my bones and rips away my feathers. In these moments, injustice is transparent, omnipresent, invisible as a breeze on hot days. And, as does the breeze on hot days, injustice travels from mouth to mouth. Slides down the throat. Travels the blue and purple highways of our veins, the length of our arms, across our thighs, and up to the corners of our temples. Heaps tiny rages into the heart, cleaving it from what remains of our innocence. Shreds that innocence into a thousand pieces. And from its destruction rises an enormous black mushroom. Injustice spreading in all its magnificence!

Palpable.

Fragrant.

Delirious.

Unbridled.

Monstrous.

Injustice hovers over death, extends everywhere. I want to grab it by its heels. Crumple it up. Crush it in my hand like an old newspaper. Stuff it into the immense mouth that is your body, shut it inside with the ghosts of all the other lives you've swallowed.

I say your body. But the truth is there are no boundaries between us. You, me, the other women. Your ghosts are my ghosts, their ghosts are yours. They no longer know where your body begins and theirs end. And in my body I carry you all.

I am. Mother. Lover. Friend. Executioner. Victim. Martyr. Warrior. Revolutionary! I rock back and forth. I whisper fairy tales. Spit out truths. You bury me beneath a mountain of secrets and then seize the locks of my hair to pull yourself from the wells.

Say my name, you know who I am!

I am the woman who lives in you. The woman you love and who loves you in turn. She who would tear out your eyes and your tongue, chop off the hands that strangled her child. She who rubs your hands to warm them and puts your bear-paw to her breast.

I am these women. They are all me. Their nightmares haunt my dreams. Their dreams invade your nightmares. I gather up dreams, I gather up nightmares, caress them, cajole them, feed them.

I am the woman who waits on your suffering. She who replays your death to savour the violence of it. Who awaits your death as she does the return of her

9

vanished child, even though she knows doing so is a lie. Grief, anger, rebirth. Lies that keep her alive.

Hush, my love, my Arik. No. Don't gouge out my eyes. Don't deprive yourself of their light, even if it burns. Here, take my heart instead. Feel me. Wander in my shadows. Light is wicked when it exists without night. It cannot be just for itself.

The light is that abundant part of me I must tone down. Dull the glare with splatters of grey and brown. The half-light that makes it possible to love the half-man half-monster. The machine crushing souls to pieces for the sake of a wall. The grieving father, the brawling son, the man who knows how to tell a joke. Go, go to where you bury your pain, your laughter, your amazements. Welcome, without remorse, your joys when they come knocking at my door. Unfetter your dreams inside me without betraying these other women.

Will they blame me if I remove the shadow from each letter of your name, the violence from each date in your biography? If I take death from you and lend you life? Will they resent me if I am able to slip in and see you, as they do, naked? If I stripped you of your many layers, your warrior's skin, your politician's mask? Until nothing is left before me but you? Until you are nobody? Until I am nobody?

Let us be no one. Let us, together, be without a face. Let us lose ourselves in this deep sleep. Lift the veils from all our faces.

Go on, ask me: what is your name? I'll name all the women.

And ask yourself: who am I? All the women will answer you. Their voices are my voice. Do you really not know who you are?

Don't cry, Arik. Get to your feet on my legs.

Let's go back. I'll come with you.

Let's go back to the very beginning.

Before me.

Before you.

VERA

Is that you, Arik? I hear your footsteps in the snow. Don't hide. The forest is bare. Come to the fire. Sit close to me. My eyesight's not what it used to be. Oh! How you've aged since I died! Has it been eighteen years already? I've lost all sense of time...

You're shivering. Come here, let me hold you. Lay your head on my chest. Don't be shy. Who knows when we'll be able to touch one another again? We've wasted enough time as it is. A whole life without hugs. Don't fight my tenderness, Arik, now that I can finally loosen the bowstring. Here. Take my coat. I don't need it. The cold and I are old friends.

Why this distance? Touch this face. These molli-fied angles, these folded eyelids, these cheeks still high despite my years. My forehead, my brows, my nose straight as the letter *I*. You love this nose. You would so like to have inherited it. Not these lips, though. Too

13

thin for your taste, you who melts before Lily's full mouth. Go on. Caress this brown skin, its patches, its wrinkles. Is it not familiar, this face? No doubt I've changed. Look at these hands. All crumpled. Worn down by farm work. These hands weren't made for milking cows. I'd always imagined them holding a stethoscope over a baby's heart. Funny, no? Does my smile surprise you? A smile of wisdom, I suppose.

You don't recognize me, do you? Neither my voice, nor even my Russian accent that makes you laugh so when I swear in Hebrew? Don't worry about it, Arik. Call me Vera. I survived the beginning and the end. And that's what you're looking for, isn't it? The beginning of all this and an end, a way out of the coma? You can die, Arik. Right now, if you want to. All you have to do is ask. I'm your *mamushka*. I gave you life. I could take it back.

What, then? You miss the sun and blue sky? You want to see them again before you die? My son, *synulya, bni hayakar*! I say that to you in all languages. Dead or alive, you belong to me. I know you, Arik. You won't be leaving here without knowing the path you left behind.

Get up now and put out the fire. Are you brave enough to face the cold? Let's walk, walk until we can't feel our toes anymore. Ah, when I was just a little thing, I used to love fluttering my eyelashes against my fingertips and seeing how stiff the snow had made them. Let's go. Give me your arm, *synulya*, let's walk to the beginning of history.

Watch out for the roots of the trees! Your ancestor planted them. What a tall, strong man he was. So tall and strong he intimidates friends and foes alike. He serves in Russia, in the Tsar's army. As a reward for his bravery, the Tsar gives him a forest at the edge of the empire, along the Dnieper River. Do you know where that is? It's my home. In Belarus. Yes, yes, I know, at the time there was no such place as Belarus. Just the Russian Empire and the forest. That's the sum of it.

You'd have thought him suffering in exile. But no. To this man, one who never expected to own land, the forest is a gift from heaven. He moves with his family to Galevencici, at the edge of the woods. There, where lights twinkle in the distance. For generations, they are the only Jews in the region. The man's name is Schneeroff and he bequeaths the forest, his woodsman's vocation, his imposing height to my father Mordecai. Then I inherit my father's stout body, his iron-like carapace, in turn. And now I, your mother, what shall I leave to you, poor Arik, eh?

No, don't answer that.

In Galevencici there's no electricity, no running water. The wooden walls of the house whistle whenever the wind is up. On winter nights my brothers and sisters and I sleep so close to the fireplace that sparks burn holes in our blankets. At dawn, the echo

15

of my father's axe inveigles its way into my sleep.

Do you hear that pounding on the tree trunk? That's the beat of my childhood.

Just as it will be in Palestine for you and your sister Dita, lost in your grammar books while outside, Shmuel, your father, rakes straw in that dump of a *moshav*, Kfar Malal.

A generation, a migration, and so many farewells between you and me, my darlings. And to what end? *Za chem*, Arik, for what? We abandon our Russian lives to live under siege in Palestine! Your father gathers straw without ever taking his eyes off the barn, for fear it will be set on fire, as I survey the horizon from the window, the Mauser close at hand.

A German rifle! German!

Jews are being killed with the same firearm in Europe and here I am, ready to shoot Arabs with my Mauser. Life can be perverse, can it not? Oh yes, it can! And you, my little *zaychik*, you run around like a little rabbit with a Caucasian dagger in your hand. A bunny barely out of the hutch, proudly brandishing the weapon your father gave you for your fifth birthday. What benefit is there in leaving war behind to build a new nation somewhere else, if you have to fight another war in order to live in it? To have to sleep with a bloodstained club underneath the bed. Leave your son on his own all night to keep watch over the fields and the hostile neighbours at their edge.

If it means not lifting a finger when he turns into an assassin, and even going so far as to rejoice in his transformation. Aged fifteen, you're already training with the youth militia. From the fields to the Haganah camps, and from the camps to the battlefields. What was the point of saving you from Russia's gangs and pogroms?

Have we really made any progress since my youth? Not an iota! What does it matter, I'm in my forest now, and you're here with me. Far away from that *such'ya* life. Oh, please! Don't look so shocked, it's not as if you've never heard me swear before. Forget I'm your mother and look at me, Arik. No, don't look away! I'm Vera. I'm a woman. I curse. And I wail!

Shhh!

There's the sound of your grandfather's axe. Good, good, all is good. He's here, everything's in order. No! Don't touch me! I'm calm now ... I apologize, *synulya*. It's been so long since I've opened my mouth to speak, a long time since I've revisited all that. Kfar Malal. Galevencici. The anguish.

The anguish of not hearing my father's axe in the morning. Mornings when the wind blows so loudly it buries the sound of his chopping. Not knowing if the sun is going to rise. If I'm to live for another day. You feel it, profoundly, the anguish. Come too soon, Arik. It's our fault. Mine, your father's. We raised you with a gun in your hand. The more I think of it, the more

I understand how much our childhoods were alike. We're nothing but mice on a wheel.

A whole life rubbing shoulders with death. Going out into the woods, following its echo. Sometimes in the songs of the birds, sometimes in the galloping of wild horses. Waiting for the day when death will come. Immersing myself in the rustle of leaves. Brooding over the conversations of the day before, the whisperings of friends come from cities filled with horror stories of Jews beaten in the streets. Odessa, Minsk, Brest.

They visit us at Yom Kippur or at Easter, the only Jews we see throughout the year. We feel less isolated when they're with us. But they arrive encumbered with bad news and never stop discussing imminent, terrible massacres! They talk excitedly about the gangs invading Odessa and sullying the reputations of the Jews. The bandits of King Benia Krik, and Phroïm Gratch, and Kolka Pakovski. We call them *shtarks*, strongmen — count on Yiddish to ennoble the mobsters who intimidate the authorities, terrorize the shopkeepers of their own people, and who, the next day, defend these same shopkeepers with fists and guns against the pogrom's hatchet men. It's enough to drive you crazy, to make you want to abandon everything. And they do abandon everything. They leave in droves, the shopkeepers and children of the Jewish ghetto. As if the arrival of the twentieth century had started a countdown. In order not to identify as exiles, they call themselves pioneers. They make *aliyah*. They haven't immigrated—no, no—they've returned to the Promised Land. When it's not gangs that drive them to Palestine, it's the hatred of their neighbours. And when it's not the hatred of their neighbours, it's the dream of being pioneers.

Not a Yom Kippur goes by without the name of Herzl echoing in the room. Yes, Arik, the same Herzl who's called *Chozeh HaMedinah*. The Visionary of the State. That brings nothing to mind? Ah! To you, to all the children of pioneers born in Palestine, he's a legend, a hero. Eyes wide as saucers, chin resting on your hands, you listen to your father tell stories of this Hungarian who realized the Utopian dream of gathering all the Jews of the world together in Jerusalem, so they might have a state and a homeland.

Eretz Yisrael. The Land of Israel!

Once you're in bed, watching the rats course along the roof-beams of the house in Kfar Malal, you repeat the word: *visionary, visionary, visionary*, as if to absorb its power. To provide yourself the strength to stand against the fear, against the horrors of the Second World War spat out of the radio day and night, against the anger of the Arabs and the spite of the English.

You wonder how I know this?

I'm your mother, Arik. When I was your age, I too had dreams, hopes, nightmares. I also dreaded the day when the tide of blood would reach us. At any rate, in this sorry shack of Kfar Malal, nothing happens without our knowing about it. Even thoughts make noises here.

A cabin built on a patch of sterile land, surrounded by a dozen others given to couples, like your father and me, foolish enough to accept being the guinea pigs of ideologues. A putrid cabin with walls built of mud and manure, shared with a mule and a cow. It's your idea to name the cow *Tikvah*. Hope! I laugh at that when I'm not crying. Two fools, a cow, a mule, and a couple of children in Kfar Malal. Oh, yes! And a dog. Crammed into a beautiful middle-of-nowhere kibbutz.

Sof ha'olam smola. Turn left at the end of the world. The only words in Hebrew that help me let off steam.

Smack in the middle of nowhere!

During the day, we stare at the baking sun; at night, at the beam that separates us from the granary and rats. You mumble the name Herzl, thinking we're asleep. Me, I never sleep.

I mull over all the things that this man has destroyed in my life. Because there's no getting around it, Arik, he's just a man. A man with a single idea. A man either lucky or astute enough to die before witnessing the consequences of his idea. In 1904, he dies. In 1921, Shmuel and I are already in Palestine, parachuted into this alien land, confronting all the pitfalls Herzl's dream did not anticipate.

During the sleepless nights of Kfar Malal, I drift far from the nauseating odour and lowing of the beasts back to Galevencici. To before your birth, to before Israel is born. Towards festive nights and my parents' house filled with visitors. Towards the dinner guests who, from the moment they take their places at the table, repeat what Herzl has said word for word, reporting on the stormy debates and disputes of the Zionist councils. In Basel. In Switzerland. The outrage when he proposes establishing a Jewish homeland in Uganda. In Uganda, of all places!

Four years after his death, Herzl is crowned as the *Chozeh HaMedinah*. Uganda? Forgotten! Everyone is looking to Palestine. That legendary territory where miracles fall from the trees. A Chosen Land for a Chosen People. A land without people for a people without land. Except no one told the Arabs already living there. Well, they were there! I'll end up with enough of their blood on my club to know. Whatever. Herzl and his disciples concocted a mix of myths and utopias irresistible to every disillusioned Jew on Earth.

Ah, those nights in Galevencici...My father nods his head. From time to time he sighs deeply as he listens to his dinner guests praising Eretz Yisrael, the place where all our problems will be resolved. One guest vaunts the donations he has made to the National Jewish Fund. Another advises my father to quit Russia as quickly as possible. Your grandparents stay out of politics. We, the Schneeroff family, know we are Jews. But never, never, not for a moment, did we ever doubt we were also

Russians. That we belonged to this forest, witness to our coming of age in its birches, climbing the tentacle-like hop vines concealing their trunks.

Touch them, Arik. In winter the vines are dry and dead, but in the spring they crawl all the way up the thin silhouettes of the forest pines and reach their tops and strangle them with their stems.

Izvinite! I'm sorry, I'm losing my train of thought... What were we talking about? Yes, yes, the dinner guests.

The dinners always end on the same note. My father thanks the guests for their generosity, then politely asks about books. Did you bring that new edition of Tolstoy? What about the Chekhov? Still can't find it? What do you have of Gogol's, or Gorky's? And so it goes until the last drop of vodka is drunk: a catalogue of writers I come across later, rummaging in my father's library. Worn out, the guests leave without quite getting a handle on my father's views, or his opinion of Herzl the visionary.

If only they'd asked me!

They depart, mouthing the traditional "Next year in Jerusalem," and the evening's names, retorts, and disagreements reverberate in the room behind them. Their words embed themselves in me, transform me without anyone paying heed. But for the Mongolian fold of my eyes, I am just one girl among seven brothers and sisters.

No one notices me at the table, or pays attention

when I leave to empty my head of their adult words.

No one sees me climb up onto the roof to gaze at the stars.

No one knows that even though I'm only five years old, and despite my fear of the world, I dream of accomplishing great things. To be a part of the stories recounted by the Yom Kippur visitors. Of the rebellions that implode as suddenly as they explode. Of the killings that carpet entire villages with blood as red as the field of poppies in front of our house. Streets filled with broken glass, with the murdered bodies of strikers and dissidents executed by the Tsarists. And if, unfortunately, you are a dissident, a striker and a Jew... *Katastrofa*!

This is before there's any talk of Bolshevik revolutions and world wars. When the workers of St. Petersburg are shot down. The time of the General Strike. Of mutiny in the port of Odessa. Demonstrations demanding a new social order. Promises of a more just constitution. And then the Tsar's vengeance. Reprisals such as have never been seen before! All in a single year: 1905. The year that puts into play the Revolution and all the wars that come after.

The Yom Kippur dinner guests turn out to be right. The Russian Empire crumbles. The same merciless Tsar ends up pleading for his own life and that of his children. In vain. They are slaughtered, one after the other, like cattle.

These events burrow into my gut like a worm in fertile soil. I want to be a part of them, even though I understand so little. Secretly, though I'm terrified by the idea of being shot at by the Tsarist army or an enraged mob, I envy those living in the rebelling towns, those who flee them for other places, and even those who are killed there. The urge to be alive even at the risk of dying, that's what I want with all my being. With the dawn of the new century, everything is possible in Russia, the best as well as the worst, and I don't want to miss any of it!

Oh, Arik, can I admit something to you, now that you're finally here with me, in this place where we owe nothing to anyone? I'm glad you've lost your memory. The Vera who emigrates to Palestine to build Israel, who raises you without ever tenderly kissing or even hugging, who does what she has to do without complaint, the woman who locks herself in her room to write long letters to friends and brothers and sisters scattered everywhere, this Vera would never truly confide in you, never have let you know the young peasant girl from Belarus who wanted to conquer the world.

Forget your mother. Forget that miserable woman exiled in the country of Herzl. I am a child of the century! Febrile. Ambitious.

1900. One-nine-zero-zero. The year of my birth is proof of it: everything starts with me. The double zero of my birthday keeps the world running on time. Measures the passing seasons. Divides history into centuries and half-centuries. A sign of destiny. A reminder of the time flashing by. Of all the great things still left undone!

Ha! Idiot. Child. Naive little girl. How could I not be a prisoner of my age, those two zeros so clearly there, so precise, so easily counted? How could I add a year or two when it suits? Or leave one or two out when old age catches up with me?

Do you find my coquetry amusing, Arik? Coquetry is a luxury I've never had the right to indulge in. My life does not belong to me but to the cycle of history. I've been at the mercy of everything it throws at me, good or bad, start to finish, right from day one.

1905: the year of pogroms and strikes, I'm five years old.

1917: the year of the Russian Revolution and the fall of the Tsar, I'm seventeen.

1921: the year I arrive in Kfar Malal, I'm twenty-one.

1928: the year of your birth, twenty-eight.

1948: the birth of Israel, I'm forty-eight.

1988: the year of my death, at eighty-eight.

I'm an echo. Empty. As full of holes as the twin zeros of my birth year.

If only I could take it all back, Arik... Be content with the hard, spartan life that was mine in Galevencici. If anyone had warned me of what awaited me in

Palestine I would never have followed your father, never have given up my medical studies. Look. All this beauty surrounding us. Far from the world. From its cruelty. To live in a village, neither poor nor unhappy. To live. Without friends, without enemies. Just live! With winter. Its silence.

Ah, *synulya*... How I missed the cold when we moved to Palestine. This dry cold that stings your cheeks. In Kfar Malal, I spend my nights dreaming about it. To be far from the humidity. To float. High. High above the Mediterranean. Above its salty air, its intolerable odour of fish. I fly back to the forest. Sweep the snow that clings to the tree trunks. Lick snowflakes off my red mittens. Return. Return to nature. Bury my feet in a blanket of white, white snow! Listen. The ice squeaks under my boots. Breaks up, refreezes. Crick, crack, crick.

You feel warmer already, don't you Arik? The forest is in you. Here, no one can hurt you. The children of the village stay out of the woods, especially the part that's ours. In school, they tell stories of a bearded giant who roams among the spruces. They mean my father. He frightens them. I'm proud of him. The fearful respect you inspire in your allies as much as your adversaries, Arik, is something you inherited from your grandfather.

The caution of the children reassures me, because I'm also afraid of them. The village is as dangerous to me as the forest is to them. I walk to school as if into battle. Ready to challenge malicious looks. To return injurious words. But my schoolmates keep their distance. No one provokes me. They're neither kind nor mean, just indifferent. And when hostility is every- where, indifference isn't such a bad thing. On the day that the pogroms strike nearby villages and towns, we are left alone. And this even though, as the only Jews in the region, we'd make an easy target. Our family isn't touched.

Wait! Let's stop here for a minute, Arik. The river is singing...it's singing to us.

I wonder now why I was so afraid of the village children. They invent rumours about my father as they would about anyone who is different. Anyone too short, too tall, too ugly, too smart. Maybe they miss their own fathers. Galevencici empties of men during the winter, when they go away for months on end to find work in the cities. Some go as far as Baku, across the wild mountains of the Caucasus. They have no choice. If they did not, the village would starve. They leave following the river.

And the women wait for them.

And the children wait for them.

Often the men they wait for never return. Like the river, they travel in just one direction. They die on the roads, in avalanches, in accidents at the factory...

My father, a landowner, never needed to migrate or

endure the sufferings workers did. I wonder if the villagers spare us the pogroms, not out of fear for us, but because my father is the only man left in the village. His presence reassures them. Or perhaps they simply don't feel part of the hysteria sweeping through the towns.

Tell me, Arik, how do we know whether the mean stares are directed at me, or at my history? Is it my haughty personality that irks them, or the way I look? If I'd let them get close to me, would they have extended a hand or shoved me away? When a fish surrenders to the currents of a river, does it know what it will find in the ocean? A bird born in a cage, does it know what it means to be free? The struggle. Always a struggle for survival. Fish or bird, that's what's in store for them. That's what I taught you.

But I was wrong, my son. I was always that trapped bird who hops about in its cage to avoid the claws of onlookers. The bird who, once freed, takes refuge in another cage out of habit.

Aha! Bread crumbs on the path. Careful! Don't step on them. Gather them up. Follow their trail back to the beginning. What was the exact moment that brought me to Kfar Malal?

Is it this crumb?

That one?

When did it all start to come apart? The day I met your father? Or later, when I agreed to marry him? Or later still, when the Red Army knocked on our door in

Tiflis and forced us to make the choice? To leave with the rest? Take our chances in a country that doesn't even exist yet?

So there it is! The bread crumb that is Tiflis. Go on. One mouthful for you, one for me. Mmm! It tastes sweet, does it not? The taste of the most beautiful years of my life ... Today we call the capital of Georgia Tbilisi, but for me it will always be Tiflis.

I'm seventeen. When I finish high school, your grandfather Mordecai asks me what I want to do with my life. The question is so unexpected I just stare at him with my mouth hanging open.

—Vera, a Jewish family from Odessa—the Babels—has asked for your hand for their son Isaac. It's time to choose, my girl. Get married, start a family, or continue your studies. This forest can protect you no longer.

I stare at my father incredulously. Perhaps I'm not as invisible as I think. Did Mordecai see me rummaging in the library for a book? Your grandfather is an exceptional man, Arik, a modern man.

—The legacy that matters is not anything you receive, but the knowledge feeding your mind. It's the only inheritance that will never abandon, betray, or imprison you.

He hammers these words into my head constantly. Your grandfather is not, as his dinner guests imagine he is, a man divorced from reality. He sees the clouds at the tops of the mountains. He who reads Gorky instead of the newspapers knows what storms lurk on the horizon. Soon the Tsar will fall and those like us, people scattered at the edges of the empire, will bear the brunt of it. The forest won't protect us from the winds of history, your grandfather knows that. We must arm ourselves. Not with guns and illusions, but with knowledge. With knowledge! Your grandfather makes sure that we have it, my brothers and sisters and me. When I tell him I want to be a doctor, he says:

—Then it's Tiflis for you.

1917. I'm seventeen. The Tsar's family massacred, there's war between those who want to seize power. With the dawn of the Red Revolution, there's no possibility of travelling to Moscow or St. Petersburg. Not even our corner of Belarus is safe from the battles and reprisals. White Monarchists versus Red Bolsheviks. Red versus Green nationalists. The Greens versus the Revolutionary Socialists. Komuchs versus Cadets versus Anarchists versus Mensheviks. There's no end to it!

The countryside is in flames. The fields are flooded with the blood of factions. And the famine, Arik, the famine! War swallows up everything. The people die of hunger when they aren't killed by bayonets. Militias ransack the farms and empty the barns. All in the name of freedom, all in the name of peace. There's never a shortage of justifications. Freedom for whom? Peace according to whom? The answers change as quickly as the weather.

The unfortunates of one or another minority fold up their tents, gather up their children, and flee by any means available. In carts, by boat, even on foot. Some to Europe. Asia. The Far East. Others to the Americas. Most take the road leading to the countries of the Caucasus.

Go! To the Black Sea.

The Caspian.

Beyond the mountains to the borders of the empire.

There, where the war won't reach you.

The shopkeepers go to Baku and Batumi. The Zionists emigrate to Palestine. But those who wish to live, truly live, they take the road to Tiflis.

Tiflis has it all. Arts, culture, science . . . It's Jerusalem, New York, Istanbul, Tehran, Beirut, Damascus. All cities, all civilizations, all peoples, rolled into one: Ottomans, Tatars, Persians, Romanians, Byzantines, Russians . . .

You think I'm exaggerating? That it's only nostalgia talking? What do you know, Arik? Hmm? For you, there's no history before Israel, before the farm at Kfar Malal, before the project of establishing a homeland for the Jews. And if it's necessary to skip a few millennia to make it happen, then so what?

He was keen on history, your father. He never missed an opportunity to tell me about Tiflis's past. He'd have recounted it to you, too, but once we were in Palestine he avoided the subject because he didn't want

to make me sad by talking about our life back then...
Those four years. Short. Too short... Our studies at
the univer —

I'm sorry! Please, forgive my tears, *synulya*. I've been
holding them back for so long, I'm drowning in them.
Happiness is so cruel! I was happy, so very happy in
Tiflis. How can I express the joy I felt the first time I
set foot on campus?

I'm in Tiflis, the Queen City of the Caucasus, the
City of All Cities! The forest seems confining to me
now. How had I not suffocated in it all those years? I'm
a giant! I hold the entire forest in the palm of my hand.
A country in miniature. A childhood in miniature, in
the snow globe I place on top of my human anatomy
papers and drawings. I contemplate the wild, young girl
I was in that all-enclosing forest and shake the globe to
make it snow, again and again, all the while conscious
of who I am presently, a woman of the world living a
real life, and free for the first time!

Oh! It's snowing, Arik. It's snowing.

Hold out your hand. Catch the snowflakes.

These are my dreams. My reasons for joy.

All my vanished joy...

Here's one: a snowflake in the shape of a star. A
window, a slice of memory. Do you see us in there, your
father and me? Yes, that's Shmuel, and that's me. Two
university students. Brimming with confidence, our
futures seem boundless. Shmuel is studying agronomy,

I'm in medicine. How beautiful am I? See me sitting on the train, my back straight, my head high, a stack of textbooks on my lap.

It's morning. I'm on my way to class. I feel his eyes on the back of my neck, a hot spot, a ray of sunlight burning my skin. I turn around. Our eyes meet. He's two rows behind me on the other side of the carriage, a young man with an oval face. Black beard and moustache nicely shaped. Round glasses, tight vest. Tall. Thin. Tie a bit crooked but a good, clean shirt.

I recognize him from a meeting organized on campus by the Jewish Students Association. He was arguing for greater political engagement rather than letting ourselves be content with community work. The Jewish students are becoming radicalized. They feel less and less Russian, choosing instead a heritage they know little about, except for religious holidays with the family and a few Yiddish expressions sprinkled in with the Russian. Hebrew? Might as well be Latin!

Poor Shmuel. At first, his zeal doesn't get him very far. He doesn't understand that a person can be Jewish without being Zionist. He grew up in Belarus, as I did, but instead of climbing pine trees he ran about the streets of Brest with other Jewish children of his age, some of them the sons of Orthodox rabbis and nationalist zealots, others orphans from the ghettos taken in by the gangs. He lives all the escapades and misadventures our Yom Kippur dinner guests recounted in Galevencici.

In his case, the stories are not simply anecdotes ending when the dinners do, but go on for entire nights. The evening begins with plans and strategies. How to hold the British to their promise of giving us Palestine. How to get the greatest number of Jews there in the shortest possible time. How to divide up the land upon arrival. How we need to revive the Hebrew language, change the names of the villages, not hire Arabs, not buy their goods. Create an exclusively Jewish economy. What is to be done if the Arab peasants refuse to leave? Or if other countries refuse to recognize the state of Israel? How do we build an army? How do we win wars? All the questions and all the solutions are on the table. The talk will go on until the sun rises over the Promised Land.

While I wander about in my forest, he runs errands for merchants warily scraping by. And when the First World War forces his family to move to Baku, he distributes pamphlets to workers coming out of the factories. As an adolescent, he volunteers for Zionist activities when he's not studying Hebrew and the Torah with his father. If he chose agronomy, it's because he wants to prepare himself for his own ascension to Eretz Yisrael, convinced men's power rises from the land, from their attachment to the soil, from the sweat of their brow. The only way to build a nation? Root oneself in the country, possess it, transform it into something unrecognizable to anyone but Jews.

No, Arik, your father never understood young lapsed Jews who spoke only Russian and lived like Russians. Who were so assimilated they responded to his passion with a shrug of their shoulders. But, note, this didn't stop him from marrying one of them! He fell in love with my strength. My determination. That's what he tells me when, in Kfar Malal, the deprivation shows too clearly on my face.

So there he is, behind me on the train, this man who treats both authorities and the student association like a bunch of slackers. He stares at me so intently that I turn away and concentrate on the seat in front of me. We exit at the same station. I head off to class. He approaches.

— You were at the association meeting. Allow me to introduce myself: Shmuel Scheinerman.

— Vera. Vera Schneeroff.

— A pleasure. I often go to the meetings, but this is the first time I've seen you.

— I really don't have much time . . .

I look down at my textbooks.

— Medicine! he says.

— Does that surprise you?

This time I look at the book he is holding.

— Alexandre Dumas.

— Do you know his work?

— Just his name. There was something by him in my father's library.

—Probably this one. An account of his voyage to the Caucasus in 1860. It's a gem. The section on Tiflis is amazing. It almost makes me want to stay here.

—You don't live in the city?

—Yes, for now.

I found out only later what he meant by that. It was as if he'd already decided I'd be his life companion and he was preparing me for our coming exile, because what for him is a kind of ascension—the *aliyah*, the rise to the mother country—can be nothing but banishment for me.

Shmuel is a practical man who proceeds resolutely to whatever he desires. He never hesitates to show his true colours, even if it means losing friends. He prefers clarity to tact, in love as in politics, and he's letting me know he has no intention of spending his life in Tiflis. He's giving me an ultimatum, even though we've only just met—and it's incumbent on me to decide! He walks with me to the faculty. Doesn't leave until he's made a date with me.

I have such admiration for Shmuel, for his intelligence, his convictions. He opens my eyes, takes me out of my cocoon, out of the forest still in my head. I have so many first times with him. First time making love, first night at the opera, so many long nights, so many discoveries. A walk in town with Shmuel is never just a walk. It's a lesson in history, geography, politics. How many of the pastel balconies in the Betlami quarter leak? How many of them need only a good strong wind to be brought crashing down upon our heads? And yet, when I'm in their shadows with Shmuel, all danger disappears. All those hours spent hiking along the Narikala Ridge that looks down over Old Tiflis? Wandering along its sinuous edge. Taking a whole day to make the ten-minute walk from Meidan Square to the foot of the cliff below the fortress. Where did she go, Arik, that sparkling young woman so much in love?

Her ashes are scattered in the streets of Tiflis.

Her heart is buried under the rubble of the Muslim observatory — sorry, *Umayyad*, Shmuel corrects me — where he kissed me as we climbed to the citadel.

Her hands caress the Persian engravings in the Academy of Arts and Letters.

Her feet tread the open market on Chonkadze Street, and the cobblestone streets of Lagidze and Shavteli.

Her eyes are riveted on the frescos in the Sioni Cathedral.

Her knees, exhausted from hurrying up hilly streets in high heels.

Hurry, Vera! He's waiting for you in front of the Imperial Theatre. Ah! The Moorish opera house. We met there so many times. So many travels. To Andalusia. To the hell of *Faust*, Shmuel's favourite opera.

That Vera is still there. Her soul in every brick, every arabesque, every tree in the Tiflis botanical garden.

These days, when anyone thinks of Georgia, Joseph Stalin, that beast, that *gruzinskiy kham*, comes to mind! The barbaric son of a barbaric country, they tell themselves. Memory is short. Tiflis existed long before that butcher. One day I'll leave the woods and return there.

Shmuel walks the streets of Tiflis the better to master them. Me, I give myself up to them with my eyes shut. They are my new forest. I feel myself among their trees. The war will not reach us in Tiflis, and even if it does catch us, I'll be a doctor and able to care for the victims. We'll spend the rest of our lives here. Man of ideas that he is, Shmuel will be satisfied dreaming of Israel. Though once our studies are completed and our family started, he'll abandon the fantasy of realizing the *aliyah* to others. Besides, what would we find in Jerusalem that we don't already have in Tiflis?

Every time Shmuel talks about emigrating to Jerusalem, this is the question lurking at the tip of my tongue, but I never ask it. He sees only obstacles and dangers ahead. He seeks answers, solutions, the most direct route to Palestine. When the Red Army arrives in Tiflis in 1921, he's almost happy. He's just received his degree in agronomy. He has the means and a pretext for leaving.

—I have two years left, Shmuel, only two years before I become a doctor.

—It's now or never!

How many times have I heard that futile phrase? For

weeks and weeks, I postpone the inevitable but the pull of the tide is too strong. The Red Army gains ground and Zionists like Shmuel, nationalists and religious fanatics too, are in the sights of their new masters. Any sovereigntist movement rising from the ashes of the old empire is crushed. Despite everything, I hang on to the hope that Tiflis will protect us. That on its canvas of a thousand stories, ours will have its place. Our future, too.

Shmuel dreams of painting his own canvas. He wants to rewrite the Jewish narrative, to reshape men and women and fashion a people out of them. What hope does my ambition to finish my medical studies and live among the Georgians have in the face of his grand dream? Anyone observing us at a distance would see two sides of a single coin. He the town, me the country: two ambitious Russians made one by the strength of their characters.

But that isn't the case.

When being Jewish obliges me to fight, I fight. For survival. To defend myself. But I never wanted to change the world. I just want to live, to take advantage of all life has to offer.

Not Shmuel.

He belongs to that race of men willing to go to war for an idea. And how seductive are such men when they set about reshaping the world with their words...

Shmuel extols the virtues of backbreaking physical labour, considers it a virtue, a vocation. Bah! Only city rats talk about country life in such terms. He's never had to chop wood, to work the soil, to haul bucket after bucket of water from the river to the house. He's read a ton of books, I'll give him that, but he's never had to shove his arm up a cow's birth canal to pull a calf, or to fork and spread manure all day long until you reek of it yourself. He's never stooped for hours, pulling weeds and examining each stem, every leaf, every insect and worm. He's never got up in the morning, his neck stiff from checking the sky for hints of the weather. He'll learn all that in Palestine. Not before.

In Tiflis, he finds the prospect of the challenges we'll face after *aliyah* exciting. Nothing can slow down the train in his head that's so rapidly approaching. At the time, it strikes me as funny, listening to his dreams of living on the land, of living thanks to the land. His imagining the exotic fruits he'll grow in Yeretz Israel, the idyllic life we'll have there. I should have set him straight, told him the truth about living in the country or on a farm, things I know so much about!

But Shmuel speaks with the arrogance and authority of a man in love with his own knowledge. He explains agronomy to me with a confidence only he possesses: nothing I know about country life is of any value, given that we're about to revolutionize everything! Deep down, I know as much. This man who has heart palpitations every time he climbs a steep hillside — and Tiflis had many. This man who never carries anything heavy. Whose nose has smelled nothing but ink and textbooks. Whose fingers are good only for pressing on the strings of a violin. This man who practises his Latin and French and German. Such a man will not make it as a peasant for long. But what can I tell you, Arik? What from anyone else's mouth has the ring of fantasy, takes on an air of inevitability when it comes from Shmuel's lips.

He has an aura that shrugs off all restraints. He floats on his grand ideas; the more robust and audacious they are, the less absurd they seem. I want to fly, too, to be free of gravity. In his company, I discover unsuspected talents in myself. He promises me that I'll complete my studies there, that once we have a piece of land in the co-op and our house is built, I'll be able to enroll at the American University in Beirut and attend to my Jewish compatriots in a country that is our own.

I believe it. Idiot that I am, I believe it.

1918: at eighteen, I love him.

1921: at twenty-one, I marry him.

For the rest of my life, I carry the world on my shoulders for the sake of this love.

He dies in 1956, at the age of sixty; the physical labour he admires so much ends up killing him. It falls to me to complete his project. Manage the farm. Combat the storms. Survive war after war. Alone. I stagger under the weight of his dream, while my own dreams are crushed beneath my feet.

Does it surprise you, Arik, that I consider my life to be a series of broken dreams?

Me, your mother.

Me, the pioneer who completes the ascension of Yeretz Israel.

Me, whose callused hands transform the sterile soil of Kfar Malal into an orchard.

Me, who hides a club beneath her bed and keeps a rifle close at hand, in case any Arab dares approach the fence around our farm.

Me, who fends off anyone who contests our right to live on the land in their place.

Me, me, me! Me, who gave my youth, my strength, to this country, who nourished it — bore its child prodigy, its protector and its king!

Does it bother you that I miss Galevencici, and Tiflis, and Russia, their countrysides, their wars, their follies? Perhaps you'd prefer still to be the little boy who spies on me through the keyhole, my head bent over the letters I write all day long? The child who, starved for affection, asks his mother why she locks herself in her room and cries over her notebooks. Why she never lost her Russian accent, never threw out her old medical manuals? Why melancholy infuses her eyes at moments of great triumph?

You were born in the Promised Land, sure of your place in Israel. What do you know of deracination, of exile? How can I explain that you're the son of a

42

disillusioned immigrant, shipwrecked in a strange land among a hostile people who neither need nor want to be remade in his image? That the fantasy of this land means nothing to a woman who wants to be a doctor, who aspires to be rich in one of the great cities of Europe? Who finds this ancient people to which she is condemned to belong entirely banal? Who recognizes herself neither in their habits nor in their features, still less in Hebrew, the archaic language they insist on reviving?

In the 1920s, Shmuel and I are in Kfar Malal, with a bit of land and nothing more, and surrounded by socialists. They expect everyone to think along the same lines. These same fools fled the Red Army and then, landed in Palestine, established a society of workers — an egalitarian society, with no rich and no poor, where everyone works for the common good. We have to bow to the dictates of Yvel, the Orchard Committee and the Workers' Party, which parcels out the land, as well as their acolytes — who irritate us with their propaganda, confiscate pieces of our property on behalf of the neighbouring colony whenever it suits them, and force us to plant orange and lemon trees instead of watermelons. All this drives Shmuel mad with rage.

He hates authority figures, hates anyone who pretends to knowledge or power or legitimacy, and especially those who think they're in the right. Ha! Obviously — *ochividno* — the only authority he acknowledges is his own. The only legitimacy is his. He's always right. *Of course.*

He's a capitalist, a conservative, and a nationalist at a time when just one party, a single vision, dominates. How do you expect them to love him? Those who wish to be included must submit to the socialists. Shmuel, well, he feels beholden to no one. But for the conviction that we have a right to the land, he has nothing in common with the other inhabitants of the moshav. He delights — and I mean *delights* — in contradicting everything his neighbours and their directors say, do, or decide. The Jewish Fund, the Centre for Agronomy, the Kfar Malal Council, it's a long list.

The number of letters he writes when you are away, detailing each battle in his "cold war" against "those in power" and "their lies"! How pale their faces are when, against all odds, he manages to be elected head of the Yvel, thus speaking for the entire village.

—Like Mephistopheles before the cross in *Faust*!

Shmuel never lacks for the right words to celebrate his victories.

Moshav? Co-op? Sharing? Bah! After you and Dita are born, your father builds a fence around our farm, the only one in the whole moshav with a padlocked gate. A matter of principle! Later, when a surveyor runs a line of barbed wire across our field to mark the portion to be expropriated, I cut the wire myself. Oh, yes, if you stand next to the sprinkler, you can expect to get wet.

I'm the one who has to do the dirty work, who is at the receiving end of hostile looks after one of your father's tirades. I am the one who must re-establish communications when Shmuel starts another one of his brawls. He gallivants all over the country, I rarely leave the village. When they're not calling me the Mongolian, because of my slanted eyes, they call me the Spartan. My days are hard, his are...

Oh. I can't breathe...

Wait, son, wait, let me get my breath back. Why have you come to me? Why are you stirring up this pain? Why? Let's sit down by the river. I need a drink of water.

Ah... That's better.

In Kfar Malal, I'm a prisoner. Your father, despite all his certitudes, is he really happy? Who knows? He manages a number of orchards besides our own. These provide him with an excuse to roam all over the territory, to escape the tension that poisons our daily lives. Breeding livestock, ploughing, working the farm — as much as he loves all of this, it's not good for his frail constitution. He's at war with himself, but too proud to admit it. What? Admit that he misses the opera or walking among the monuments and relics of Tiflis? Never! On those infrequent evenings when friends drop by with their instruments to accompany him on the violin, nostalgia washes over his face, his tired body leaps to life, and his tenor's voice resounds.

Your father is a painter too — do you remember the landscapes he paints? No, Arik, not even that? Too bad. During his sixteen-hour days, he always finds a moment to slip away and paint. This split between man and peasant, or the Spartan woman and her medical calling, is sometimes unbearable. We're the first to have a radio. We follow the news of scientific advances and, of course, political events such as the rise of Stalin and the Nazis. Our interest in whatever is going on beyond the borders of the co-op, or in the country yet to be built, perplexes the other moshavniks. When we do not strike them as disagreeable, they consider us simply bizarre. The fact that we live on the same moshav makes no difference. On the contrary. It underscores our differences even more.

If the neighbours plant oranges and lemons, we plant clementines and avocadoes. After the harvest, our fruit isn't conveyed with the rest, isn't sold with the rest, or even packed the same way. Shmuel insists on beauty.

— The eye eats before the stomach.

That's the only Arabic proverb he allows himself to repeat. He insists we pack the clementines with their green leaves. Eventually everyone does it that way, but at the time he's the only one to do so and it drives the others crazy.

When it comes to voting on one thing or another, Shmuel always opposes the majority stance — and I vote with him, of course. And when he loses an argument at the Council, he simply ignores the resolution and does what he wants! Over time, a wall rises between us and the other moshavniks. Arguments and betrayals are constant. Virtually all my days begin this way, fixing crockery broken by your father, when I'm not breaking it myself. The hatred of our supposed allies and compatriots, added to that of the Arabs around us. How do you think I ended up with this thick skin for a body?

—We have to do this today, before tomorrow, we must!

We have to do this, we have to do that! With Shmuel, everything is imperative, everything is a matter of principle. And what about the damage caused by these principles of his, eh, Arik? You have suffered so much, my poor boy, from his allergy to diplomacy. I watch you from the window, arguing with the neighbour children. They spit in your face when they speak of me or your father. Never invite you to their homes. Never reply to your invitations. Shmuel lectures you when you come home with a black eye. I watch from afar as you fight back the tears. I sense everything you wish you could say. Why do they hate us, *Papachka*? Why? Why!

I should have helped you, taken you into my arms, given you a few hugs and told you what I was feeling inside, but I was never able to do that. I lacked the courage. Instead of coming to you, I hide in the bedroom and write letters—to my friends, to my loved ones, to the life I left behind and all my abandoned happiness. I lock myself away instead of opening myself up to you. Oh, my dear boy, *synulya*...With just a little love, perhaps you wouldn't have become such a glutton, starved for war and bloodshed. You might have studied history or agronomy instead of taking up a military career. You're more than the bulldozer that only knows how to destroy, a manipulator who pulls the strings, a seeker of vengeance who kills without remorse. How I loved unexpectedly finding you lying in the cornfield, smiling at the nightingales, or wiping away the tears from your eyes at the birth of a lamb. What happened to us, my son? When did we become such effective warmongers?

The river flows and flows...how pure the water is...I miss the days when I could lie down nearby, sleep under the birches without being haunted by ghosts.

At night I hear the sound of choirs singing mass from deep in the woods, of church bells ringing at noon, of hymns in the synagogue. Or is it the ululation of owls? As others nap, I take hot baths in Tiflis's Muslim Quarter. The mosque of the Azeris calls me to prayer. A welcome and a reproach. Where are you, Vera? Why did you leave us? Why are you angry with us?

The snow has stopped falling.

Here we are at the border. Can you feel the warm air coming from across the river? Do you recognize the tang of salt? Let's go back, quickly, I'm feeling nauseous.

What are you waiting for, Arik? Come on! Follow me. The road to Galevencici is over here.

Do you want to leave the forest? Go back to Kfar Malal? Why on earth? They hate us there, and I don't just mean the Arabs, though God knows they have reason enough. I'm talking about the other moshavniks. No one likes us, Arik. No one! Not the Arabs. Not the Jews on the moshav. Because of your father and his arrogance. Because of me and my disdain for the vulgar settlers jabbering away in Yiddish and mocking my Russian. Oh yes, they hate us, Arik, Jews and Arabs alike!

You know, Arik, that during all those years we spent organizing a militia to defend our farms, no one ever asked why peasants, brown-skinned like us, who ploughed their land the same way as us, who harvested fruit and raised livestock the way we did, why they were so angry with us. On whose land were we living, exactly? How did we acquire it? And your father, fobbing me off with his theories:

— *Ha-aretz, ba'aretz*, he kept saying over and over, like a parrot.

That is his only answer to your awkward questions, yours and Dita's. Truths only children are able to express. He takes a deep breath and slowly, deliberately, explains:

— We Jews have a divine right to live "on the land" . . . *ha'aretz*. Arabs are entirely welcome to live here "in the land"... *ba'aretz*... but no, they have no right *to* the land. We accommodate them, even grant them rights, but only one people can have dominion over the land, and that's us, children. *Ha'aretz*!

Oh, how baffled are your faces! Especially when you ask what point there is in buying the land if we already own it? Well, to say we have bought it and laugh at the idiot Arab peasants who understand nothing of the transactions between the rich and the settlers, between imperialist Turks and English, between, between, between...

I pity them. For their ignorance, for their innocence. When they finally wake up and start fighting back, you know what? I pity them even more. Just as you'd pity a dying man who swings his fists at nothing. You watch him until he exhausts himself, waiting for him to fall. Of course they detest us, and I detest them, too, our Arab neighbours, even though all my life all I've ever wanted was to love and be loved in return. They deserve everything that has happened to them because we're more intelligent, stronger, craftier, more desperate. We have everything to gain and nothing to lose.

Go on, Arik! Go to Kfar Malal! You'll see how they too mock us. But I'm staying here. I've been looking for myself these last eighteen years and what have I found? Rottenness. I have some weeding to do.

What's that expression I see? Remorse? Regret? Say something. Say...

—I'm sorry, *Mamachka*, so sorry that you've wasted your life for my father's sake, for mine, for my sister's— for an idea that causes such suffering to so many people, and most of all to you.

But you're leaving all the same, aren't you? For Kfar Malal, to Israel, to your cherished country? Well, you're going alone. You'll not take me into exile as your father did. Go! Become what that country makes of everyone who lives there: an assassin, begrudging, miserable. Every man and woman living there has blood on their hands. From defending themselves, from buying the peace, from their own imposition. Whatever the reason, the result is the same: betray, hate, kill. In order to exist.

The first lesson in medicine: *Primum non nocere*. First and foremost, do no harm. Those are the only Latin words I know, the only words that matter, and I have betrayed them!

When regret gnaws at me, I lie even to myself: I say, no, Vera, you're one of the Chosen People, you were selected to realize the great dream. You're right, Vera, you're always right. Stop worrying. Sleep, be calm.

Forget who you were.

Forget the little girl who counts the stars.

Forget the forest pines.

Forget your father's axe.

Forget the snow.

Forget Galevencici.

Forget Tiflis.

Forget medicine.

Forget the walks.

Forget the solitude.

Forget the arguments.

Forget the clementines.

Forget Shmuel.

Forget Dita.

Forget Arik.

Forget war.

Forget victory.

Forget the land.

Forget *ha'aretz*.

Forget *ba'aretz*.

Ha'aretz.

Ba'aretz.

Ha'aretz.

Ba'aretz.

Ha'a — what's that sound!

Quick, quick, the rifle! Where is it, where's my rifle?

Shadows in the woods.

They're coming!

Who ... who are you?

Speak! Speak up or I'll put a bullet in your head!

Who are you? Answer me!

No! Don't come any closer!

Stay back, you ghoul! Stay back or I'll shoot, you dirty Arab!

This is my forest, *my* forest!
Get out of here!
Get out! Get out! Get out!
In the river! In the river!
I'll shoot! I'll shoot! I'll shoot!

ARIK

The piano sings a melancholy tune. The notes float
in the air. Arik would reach for the melody if only . . .

Every time, it's the same. He hears the music. Then,
voices to which he's never quite able to attach a name:
the doctor giving advice, the sing-song of the nurse,
the physiotherapist using simple words to explain the
exercises. The voices rise and fall, in and out of his
consciousness. And then the music returns. Inviting,
throwing him a lifeline. But the thread of the melody
escapes him.

—What are you doing? a voice asks.

—Just lowering the volume a bit.

—No, don't touch the music.

—Gilad, it's the third time this piece has played, Uri
says. I know it's Mozart, but even Arik must be tired
of it by now.

He lowers the volume.

No. Leave it! Leave it!

The music recedes into the mist. Specks of light and shade. The darker spots dance. Become more defined. Resemble eyes. Mouths.

They're speaking to me. Who is it?

The hospital room takes shape. Corners, walls. The grey light of the ceiling, the yellow lampshade of the light on the side table. It illuminates a face at the bedside.

—Arik, it's Uri. Can you hear me? Come on, old friend, when are you going to end this strike of yours? Those cretins in the Knesset are really screwing things up in your absence.

Uri.

Arik would like to sit up. To hold this man talking to him like a brother in his arms. Tell him: I'm here.

A pain in his chest. Images.

Vera. The forest. Snow. The rifle.

She assassinated me! My mother shot me in the chest!

—Gilad! Your father's eyelids are flickering!

A tear runs from the corner of Arik's eye. A hand strokes his left cheek, wipes away the tear. Gilad emerges from the mist.

—Don't worry, *Aba*. You're fine. You're doing great.

Gilad gives him news of his health, as though talking about a friend who lives far away. Tenderly, he sponges his father's forehead with a warm cloth as he utters the terrifying words. Heart attack. Hemorrhage. Coma. Surgery.

—I'm calling the nurse.

—Thanks, Uri. Ask for the Nightingale.

—Who?

—They'll know who you mean.

—Okay. Then I'll have to leave, I'm late for a meeting. If he wakes up—

—I'll let you know right away. Don't worry.

Since the stroke, his plunge into unconsciousness, the innumerable operations, Arik's condition is relatively stable. He even shows signs of life. He opens his eyes when he hears Gilad's voice. His expression is vague, but Gilad is certain his father recognizes him.

A few weeks earlier, Gilad surprised a nurse sitting by his father's bed with a book in her hands.

—What are you reading to him?

—The memoir of a soldier in the 1948 War.

—You mean the War of Independence. My father was almost killed in it.

—He's not dead.

—You call this being alive?

—He's somewhere else.

—Will he be the same man he was if he ever wakes up?

—Miracles are possible.

Delicate features, her blonde hair in a ponytail, skin the colour of straw. A woman of ageless, evanescent beauty.

She places the book atop a pile of others.

—Hang on. Can I see it?

—If you like.

A bilingual edition. Arabic and Hebrew. The author, S. Yizhar, a Jew. The title, *Khirbet Khizeh*, is the name of an Arab village.

—Which language are you reading it in?

—Does it matter?

And she leaves.

We nicknamed her the Nightingale, one of the doctors would later tell him.

—Why is that?

An embarrassed pause.

—She, uh, looks after the serious cases.

—The Nightingale—ah, like Florence Nightingale. I get it.

—She's the one who insisted we turn on the television. She even gave the assistant a list of your father's favourite programs.

How would she know his favourite programs? What did it matter? The doctors noticed a reaction. Gilad is no longer the only one who believes that Arik remains present, maybe even screaming at them from within his inert body.

The hemorrhage had terrible complications, but his organs are intact. Neurologists, resuscitators, physiologists, massage therapists, kinesiotherapists; a whole team experiments with different treatments and therapies. Some stimulate his brain with electric shocks, others place his favourite food under his nose — grilled stuffed fish, Hungarian dumplings soaked in butter, pâtés of all sorts and flavours. Meals for which Lily had a gift and that Arik loved so much. The slightest movement of the "Sleeping Giant" — the name the hospital staff have given him — is scrutinized and analyzed.

When, a few months after Arik's coma, war breaks out in Lebanon between Israel and Hezbollah, the Nightingale takes issue with the doctors worried about the effect violent images of the fighting might have on him. They recommend documentaries about nature, classical music — in particular, Mozart, his favourite composer. More so, his beloved wife Lily's.

— The nurse is right, says Gilad. *Aba* would be furious if we kept him from following the news.

Lily, Gilad's mother, is the one who loves music and art. It was she who introduced Arik to the pleasure of listening to Mozart. Until then, only war excited him. But thanks to Lily, he becomes reacquainted with the pleasures of his childhood: his father playing the violin in the evenings, or humming a few lines of opera on their way to the market.

On Saturdays, Gilad's wife Inbal and their children visit Arik. Inbal brings flowers picked on Sycamore Farm. A refuge. The place where Arik indulged his earliest passions: agriculture and animal husbandry. He and Lily spent the most beautiful years of their lives on this farm bordering on the Negev. Inbal sets the bouquet of anemones in a vase across from the bed. The children replace the family photographs in the room with alternate ones. Arik shouldn't have to stare at the same faces week after week.

Two of the photographs have never left the Sycamore Farm living room—one of Vera standing in sunlight, her face tanned and her white hair slightly lifted by the wind, and one of Lily in jeans, standing beside a wooden fence with horses grazing in the background.

—I have a surprise for you, *Aba*.

Gilad shows him the photographs of his mother and grandmother. Suddenly, a stir. Is Arik moving a finger? His eyes glimmer. The doctor hurries into the room.

—A reflexive reaction, he declares after running a series of tests. It doesn't necessarily mean he's regaining consciousness.

Then, to soften the blow, a touch of hope:

—You know, Gilad, the human brain is a vast mystery. We've barely scratched the surface. Anything is possible.

With these words, the doctor leaves the room.

As the Nightingale approaches the bed, she casts a distinct silhouette in the neon-lit room.

—Does he hear us? Gilad asks, staring intently at his father.

—Maybe. Maybe not.

—Does he understand what we're saying?

—We should behave as if he hears and understands us.

Gilad places the photograph of Vera in front of his father.

The cardiac monitor goes berserk.

Erratic beats of the heart. Blood pressure in freefall. The alarm goes off. Red and green alerts light up the screens. The guard posted outside the room bursts in, his gun pointed at the machine. A flurry of footsteps in the hall. Before Gilad is even able to grasp what's going on, he and the guard are ushered out by the nurses and emergency personnel. Vera's framed photograph falls to the floor and is kicked like a football between the feet of the medical team. Arik is rushed into surgery.

Gilad, his head bowed, waits in the family room of the intensive care unit. One hour. Two. Three. Four... He loses all sense of time. Then suddenly she's there, the woman with the bird's name, ghost-like but strangely reassuring. She rescues the picture in its broken frame from the waste basket. The glass falls away, revealing Vera's face.

—Here... I'm so sorry.

Gilad takes it from her.

—Thank you.

He kisses the pale image of his grandmother.

—What's happening to *Aba*, *Verochka*? Where is he? Who's he with? Why did he react like that?

The photograph does not respond.

—His routines are unchanged, his health is good. No bedsores, no blood clots, no pneumonia...zero complications. You see, *Verochka*? I've become a medical expert. You always wanted me to be a doctor. Everything was going so well for *Aba*. So, why?

—Gilad.

Uri Dan is standing in front of him, appears drawn. No sign of the Nightingale.

—Uri...

Of all Arik's friends, Uri Dan is the one most devastated by his mishap. Never has there been a closer relationship between a politician and a journalist. The Legend of Ariel Sharon was born thanks to Uri, and Uri would never have become the war correspondent he is now without Arik. One day in 1954, just nineteen years old, Uri the journalist walks into Arik's office unauthorized. He's audacious, brimming with energy. He wants to participate in the raids on Arab territories and become a war correspondent. Arik, lieutenant colonel, twenty-six, tells him he needs to undergo basic training, become a parachutist and an officer; he's certain the diminutive guy will be exhausted by the training and stop bothering him. But Uri comes back! He spends two years with the troops, at the heart of the reprisals against the Palestinian guerillas in the Gaza Strip and the West Bank led by Sharon, who's been promoted to full colonel. It's the start of a long friendship.

When Uri is scorned for his lack of objectivity, Uri laughs.

—Nothing will ever make me say anything bad about Arik!

Uri's declarations of loyalty have always boosted my father's morale, never more so than when the rest of the world was clamouring for his head, thinks Gilad. He stares at the journalist, who'd rushed to the hospital the moment he heard about the stroke. Now, what with Arik in a coma, Uri is an orphan, disoriented, depressed, unable to accept what's become of a man invincible in his eyes. It was Uri who crowned Arik "the King of Israel" after his crossing of the Sinai during the 1973 war against Egypt. Even the Palestinians recognize his power. He is the worst of enemies. Arik occupies a formidable place in the nightmares of their forced exile and their uprooting, in the heroic stories of a people persecuted.

The bulldozer!

The Butcher of Beirut!

Nicknames that secretly please Arik.

—Better to be feared than liked.

That's what Uri tells him whenever he senses the old lion wavering, or when a measure of doubt flickers across his features—as it did most notably in 1982, after Sabra and Shatila.

Massacre, cries the international press!

War crime, shout the Palestine sympathizers!

Monster, claims the whole world!

And as the Israeli political elite, that band of blood-suckers, bad-mouth their own general and minister of defence, as they salivate over the recommendation of the Kahan Commission of Inquiry into the Events at the Refugee Camps in Beirut that Arik be relieved of his duties, Uri defends his friend with every weapon his profession has placed at his command.

— *Men, women, and children shot and hacked to death. Pregnant women eviscerated!*

— Arafat has only himself to blame for daring to raise arms against Israel.

— *Christian Phalangists unleashed upon the refugees!*

— It's their civil war. What does it have to do with us?

— *You armed them, you trained them, you invaded the country and handed them the camps on a platter!*

— That's called military strategy.

— *Who sent the Tzahal into Beirut?*

— Ariel Sharon. So?

— *Who left such a trail of blood and destruction?*

Ariel Sharon, the only one who never made a secret of his intentions: Arafat, the PLO, they had to be liquidated. And if he'd not been prevented from eliminating Arafat in Beirut, then we wouldn't have had to deal with that snake in Oslo. Why be content with peace when we can have victory?

The man facing Gilad is a shadow of his former self. Uri is seven years younger than Arik but, since his friend's illness, age has ravaged his features.

—Any news?

—He's still in the operating room.

Gilad hands him Vera's photograph.

—She was quite a woman! He's alive today because of her. A hard mother in tough times who raised a tough man.

—But at what price, Uri? They made a monster of him.

—Is it such a bad thing to be a monster among monsters?

Gilad wishes the world knew the *bon vivant*, the gentle parent who never missed a chance to embrace him, and not the belligerent politician ready to bring everything crashing down on a whim; the farmer assiduously naming each avocado tree and lamb on the farm; the soldier resolutely blowing up houses over the heads of Arabs. In the run-up to the elections, the leftist press reminds citizens of every vice his father had, every mistake he has ever made, even implicating him in the trouble Gilad's brother Omri is having with the police—his violation of party financing laws, falsification of documents and perjury. Arik refuses to throw his eldest son to the wolves but, instead of seeing an exemplary father's devotion for what it is, the media use the opportunity to tarnish his reputation! Gilad promises to one day write a memoir of his father that will nail shut the mouths of his detractors once and for all.

—I don't care, *Aba*, whether you're complicit in Omri's shenanigans or not. Whether you're a murderer or not, whom you have killed and how. I don't care! Wake up, that's all I ask.

Gilad's entreaties remain stuck in his throat. Arik is in the operating room. Nothing to do but wait and bring everything to light.

At the beginning of the electoral campaign, Finkelstein, the American campaign adviser, suggests Arik might improve his public image by playing on his status as a grandfather and family man. Gilad likes the idea. But Uri, like all who worship Sharon, the powerful and intransigent general, is indignant.

—*Grandfather of the Nation?* Really?

Tired of the revolts rising against him from the heart of the party he founded thirty years before, Arik slams the door on the Likud. Although the general population supports the move, the reaction within the political arena is one of scorn. The bulldozer bulldozes his own party! The only antidote to his reputation as a hothead is to put his greying hair on display: make a virtue of his advanced age instead of having him compete against the young. Play the experience card. Exploit the empathy that accrues to the father figure, especially one surrounded by grandchildren.

The ruse works. The polls prove it. The result is incontestable: Kadima, the new party on the block, wins the election.

—Uri, says Gilad, breaking the silence. You remember, at the beginning of the campaign? Finkelstein was right.

Aghast, Uri sets Vera's photo down.

—The election turned your father into an innocuous old man. And now look at him, lying on a bed and letting himself be cut up by surgeons as others profit from his victory!

—That's not the point. My father's fighting for his life because of his temper and his voracious appetite. But people love him for that.

No, not for that. These vulnerabilities contradict everything Uri knows of Arik—Sharon the combative and audacious risk-taker! They contradict the story the journalist has been telling for his entire career. The Sleeping Giant, the nurses call him. What a farce! He, Uri Dan, who created an unshakeable, foundational myth of him. Myths are eternal. Surely they cannot end in such a pitiful manner. Can they?

In the beginning, Uri came to the hospital pretty well every day, convinced Arik would soon wake up and make a mockery of all their sad faces.

—Had you, didn't I! I just needed a bit of a rest, that's all. In this country, you have to play dead to be left alone.

What would Uri not give to hear that mocking voice now...

—Wake up, Gilad, your father's legacy is in peril.

In April, the cabinet declared him totally and permanently incapacitated. Unanimously, Gilad. *Totally and permanently incapacitated.* Who's running the show now? Ehud Olmert!

Uri never understood what Arik saw in that man. Since the onset of Arik's coma, Olmert has committed the country to a war against the Hezbollah that's being lost on every front. He has succeeded neither in destroying the Lebanese militia nor recovering the soldiers captured by them!

— But Arik, what are you doing, wasting your time in an ICU? 2006, that was your year!

Uri's voice echoes in the hallway, Gilad's sigh the only reply.

Ever since the retreat from Gaza, Arik's ways have been harder to fathom.

Establish settlements to control the territory. Never, ever surround Israel with walls or solid borders. Leave a way open for expansion. Present the Palestinians, and the rest of the world, with a *fait accompli.*

One war at a time.

One settlement at a time.

One bulldozer at a time.

This was Arik's vision, one he would defend his entire life.

But then, suddenly, he withdraws from the Gaza Strip. Dismantles the settlements. An about-face Uri can't understand. Arik can talk all he likes about the reasons behind his decisions: Bush's declaration against the right of return of the millions of Palestinian refugees uprooted in 1948 in favour of maintaining large blocks of Israeli settlements on the West Bank. An American "road map" towards a resolution of the conflict that was made-to-measure for Israel—and which, moreover, mulls Uri, short-circuits international law, the Geneva Convention, the Universal Declaration of Human Rights, and the resolutions of the United Nations. All the judicial apparatus that has been a thorn in Israel's side for seventy years. This, using a favourite term of Arik's that he'd inherited from his father, is "practical Zionism" at work.

But pragmatism has never been Uri's strong point. If there's one thing he understands, it's the power of the image. Jewish soldiers dragging Jewish settlers off expropriated land? An intolerable image. Uri does all he can to dissuade his friend. But Arik is stubborn, and refuses to budge from his position.

—We're talking about four hundred agricultural holdings, no more. And they'll be compensated.

Uri never thought he'd find himself writing a negative word about Arik. And now he's taking issue with him in their discussions as well as criticizing him in his articles. For his report on Israel's Channel One, he wears an orange tie to signify his solidarity with the settlers. Arik, who never misses one of Uri's appearances on television, flies into such a rage he turns off the set. Usually, Uri receives a phone call from Arik after an appearance. This time, no phone call. It takes the mediation of a mutual friend and the promise he'd made to Arik's mother Vera never to burn bridges to save the friendship.

All that happened a year ago but 2005 seems a decade away now. Uri can't help connecting Arik's stroke to his ideological weakening. A slippery slope, it is: frailty engenders frailty. The stroke is hard on everyone, but for Uri it's a political as much as a personal defeat. His career is inextricably tied to that of his friend, the man who represents all that is best about Israel: strength, audacity, power.

His visits to the hospital taper off, but not a day goes by without his checking on Arik's condition, either with Arik's doctor or with Gilad. From time to time he brings his notebooks and reads Arik excerpts from their numerous interviews. Fifty years of conversations. The book is published, but what good does that do? Arik's not there to congratulate his confrère.

Uri has a fit of coughing.

— You're making me sick with worry, old friend. If you don't wake up, I'll soon be joining you.

Steps in the corridor. The surgeon approaches, accompanied by the Nightingale.

— Give us some good news, Doctor.

— Mr. Sharon is alive, but … we had to remove a third of his large intestine.

Silence.

—He's alive, Gilad, murmurs the Nightingale. Alive.

—For how long...

—It's up to him to decide when to die.

Arik is returned to his room. In Gilad's and Uri's eyes he still seems silent, inscrutable, while in fact he's struggling to make himself heard.

I'm here. I'm here. I'm here!

—*Aba*, the operation went well. Inbal and the children are coming up with falafels garnished with pickled eggplant, the kind you...

Gilad stops talking. His father no longer has a digestive tract with which to enjoy his favourite foods.

I don't have enough intestine.

The realization pulses through the room. From Gilad to Arik to Uri to Gilad to Arik. Clear. Indisputable.

Arik breathes. Inhales through his nose. Exhales through the hole Vera's bullet left in his chest. Air leaves him. Everything escapes him. The music. His breath. His voice. He empties himself out. Closes his eyes, curls in on himself as though tying a knot. Anything to plug the hole.

—Okay, okay, so there's a hole in your chest. But what's one hole considering all you went through in Latrun? The Arabs practically castrate you in '48 and yet you survive. You fall to the ground, bleeding profusely. You lose the battle and half your troops. But faced with death you arise stronger than ever! You form Unit 101 and take your revenge.

Uri is perorating. Telling stories. Saying anything, it doesn't matter what. Anything but this silence and the unequivocal conclusions it brings on.

— Arik, squeeze my finger if you can hear me.

He squeezes and squeezes the journalist's index finger. To no avail.

— Uri, even if he is conscious, he won't have recovered from the surgery. Let him rest.

— I saw his eyelids move.

— The doctors say those movements are involuntary.

— What, you believe the doctors now, Gilad?

No! I'm here. I can hear you. I can feel you. I feel your hand, Gilad. I feel your little finger, Uri. Talk to me about Unit 101.

— Arik?

Yes! Yes!

— Arik.

That voice.

He gathers all his strength. Opens his eyes. Uri. Gilad. And behind Gilad, he sees her. The woman-voice talking to him from the shadows. Where has she come from?

— Arik.

Don't they see her? Gilad! Uri! She's right there!

— His eyes are open, Uri, it's true. Is he seeing angels? The dead?

— It doesn't matter. As long as he's not seeing enemies.

Not enemies. Only her. Don't go. Don't leave me alone with her!

—Arik.

The softness of her voice makes him shiver. His pupils quiver. Right. Left. Everywhere but in that woman's direction. A moment ago, she was wearing his mother's face. His mother was chasing him, firing a bullet into his chest.

—Don't be frightened, Arik.

Who is this woman?

—Why won't you look at me? Haven't I done everything you've asked? Haven't I brought you to the beginning of the story?

Who is she?

—Say my name. You know who I am.

She's speaking so loudly. Her voice tears him from that universe he wants so much to return to, where he can be with his children and his grandchildren again. Where once again he is the strong man, the warrior, the old lion, the bulldozer, and yes, the butcher. Why not all the characters Uri created for him. All except the sleeping giant.

—Arik, you don't belong in that other world anymore. Your lips are dry.

She is sitting on the edge of the bed. On the nightstand is a pile of books and a bowl filled with snow. Is the bowl still there?

—It's from the forest.

She slides a spoonful of snow into his mouth. Its freshness feels good. Colour returns to his cheeks.

She wipes his forehead.

Where did they go? Uri has disappeared. Gilad has disappeared.

—Arik, be calm, she says. Be calm. What you're seeing isn't what they see. There is here and there is there. And you are neither here nor there.

Where is he? Where?

—In the void.

Where is she? Where is she from?

—From you.

She dips the napkin in the melting snow and presses it against his forehead. The icy water runs over his eyelids, down his nose, into the furrows of his wrinkled face.

The coolness invading his skin overwhelms him. The water runs and runs. Faster. Stronger. Overflows his bed. Spills onto the floor. Rises up the walls. Submerges the room. The furniture floats. The current gurgles, then growls. Colourless swirls of foam.

She's drowning me. She's drowning me!

—Dive, Arik.

He's in the river.

Vera. His mother. The rifle.

The image assails him.

Swallows him.

Vera. The rifle. The forest.

Vera. The bullet. The river.

The shot that knocked him into the river.

Water, ice cold against the blood that seeps from his stomach. The forest sweeps by alongside the river. Amid the bare trunks of the pine trees, his mother's silhouette, the rifle brought to her shoulder, barrel still smoking. Vera shrinking as the rapids carry him away.

No, I will not die like this!

He flails his arms. His legs.

Swim. Swim. Swim!

He orders himself. Consoles himself. Castigates himself. Anything to stay alive.

Something grabs his heel. Pulls him under. The water rises. The strip of blue sky narrows. He stretches his neck, stretches a hand up to put an end to the flood. Water swallows the sky. Fills his mouth. His throat. His nostrils. His eyes.

There's no horizon anymore. Everything is floating around him.

Tentacles wrap around his legs.

Arms, hands, fingers grip his thighs.

The water churns.

Images surface.

Rivers.

Valleys.

Cliffs.

Detonations.

Screams.

Villages.

Wreckage.

Bodies.

Walls.

Streets.

Craters.

—Arik!

The woman's voice echoes in the water.

—Count the years. Count the deaths: 1948... '53...
'56... '67... '71... '73... '82... '87... 2002... 2005.

He kicks to the surface like a man crazed.

—Breathe!

He gulps a lungful of air. The current sucks him
back to the bottom of the river.

—Count the villages. Count the battlefields,
Arik. Deir Yassin. Kafr Quasem. Qibya. Suez. Sinai.
Jerusalem. Golan. Beirut. Qana. Ramallah. Gaza!

He coughs.

—Breathe!

The tentacles let go of him. To the light. Open lips.
Quickly.

Oxygen. Oxygen!

—Count the camps, Arik. Jadaliyya. Khan Younis.
Rafah. Balata. Jenin. Sabra. Shatila. Nahr al-Bared. Ain
al-Hilweh. Al-Yarmuk. Zarqa. Burj al-...

His lungs. Contract. Explode. The air escapes him.
From his nostrils. From his mouth. Bubbles, bubbles
everywhere! They fuse together. Coagulate. Form yet

more tentacles that wrap around and enchain him. Then it starts again.

Tossed to the surface.

—Breathe!

Sucked to the bottom.

Drowned. Spat out. Swallowed. Spat out again.

—Count the settlements, Arik. Ten... Twenty... Forty... Sixty... Eighty. A hundred... A hundred and twenty... A hundred and forty... Count the barriers. The lands. The olive trees, uprooted. The fields, torched. Count them. Count them. Count them!

Her voice presses and presses against his body. His bones crack. His lungs are crushed.

He is seaweed.

Suddenly, a rock.

Desperately, he latches onto it. Rubs up against its stone face. Kicks his legs. Anything to shake off the tentacles. The tearing of his skin. His legs sucked to the point of bleeding. It's him or the monster. Better to be flayed to death than to let himself be devoured. One after another the tentacles loosen. They float randomly for an instant before being carried off by the river.

He pushes to the surface. The bank is not far, but the current is too strong and he's too weak.

—Arik!

The voice comes from the edge of the water. A dark silhouette against the sun. A woman's silhouette.

—Arik!

It's her. Still her. The woman-voice throws him a rope.

—Grab the rope!

Arik clings to the rock as if to life itself.

—Are you ready to die? Let yourself go, Arik. Close your eyes, let go of the rock.

He clings harder to the rock.

—Do you want to know who I am? Grab the rope!

She throws it to him a second time and Arik seizes it, lets himself be pulled through the rapids.

The closer he comes to shore, the warmer the water is. The current slackens. The air is welcoming. The light is sweet. He moves forward, forward some more, his exhausted body following the voice. Arms pull him from the water. He collapses onto the wet ground.

—Arik. Years pass. 2006, 2007, 2008 . . . Arik! Time flies . . . 2009, 2010 . . . The blood flows. Do you want to die?

No. He doesn't want to die.

Suddenly, a shadow. The whinny of a horse. The comforting smell of straw and sweat. Of skin warmed by the sun. A ridge impregnated with dust. The smell of manure coloured purple by wild hyacinth. Odours of his childhood.

He is lifted up, lightly, into the clouds. He floats. Rocked by the horse's gait. No more river. No more blue. Sand surrounds him. And rocks. A red horizon. A dark sky.

—She's waiting for you in the cave.

The woman's voice reverberates, echo upon echo. Blends with the drip-drip of water. With the steady beat of the horse's hooves.

Then...Silence.

The air is humid. The earth mineral. Volcanic organ pipes. Copper. Bronze. The odours of the desert.

The horse sets him down.

He sinks into a deep sleep.

LILY

How handsome you are when you're sleeping, my love. I can count on the fingers of one hand the times you've snored this peacefully beside me. You think that by buying Sycamore Farm you'll find peace. That this pitiful patch of farmland in the middle of the desert will cure your insomnia. That working it will take away the filth of the city. That raising animals will save you from the toxicity of politics.

—Lily, I'm offering you the largest canvas in the world. Paint us a paradise!

I let my dreams run away with themselves. My painterly intuitions. My decorating talents. I plant roses and anemones. Red. White. Yellow. Violet. You erect a surveillance tower on the roof of the farmhouse, with a view of the surrounding countryside. Ever the soldier. Binoculars. Always on guard. Always your thumb on the ground. The hills. The valleys.

You declare to the distant mountains:

—Judea and Samaria, I'm here!

Battle lines.

Routes to furrow versus routes to follow.

Flags on the peaks awaiting settlements.

From up on top, a thousand strategies form in your head. You rush down the stairs. Just by the way you shout out, *my love*! I know. With impatience, with excitement. I know. It's time to draw up a list.

How many diplomats, generals, and politicians have we welcomed to the farm? Wooing them, making sure each has his audience? Putting them at the heart of our plans? Their presence insults and exults me at the same time.

Respectable men assiduously presenting themselves. Democrat. Diplomat. Revolutionary. Popular leader. Each has a particular manner, a particular brand. None of them want to shake hands with Ariel Sharon, the Butcher of Beirut. But they're happy enough to share our table in a discreet and intimate gathering. To explain from aperitif to dessert why they can't acknowledge their loyalty publicly. How it amuses and appalls me to listen to them. Especially the Arab leaders. I gauge their lack of power and conniving by their compliments and false indignation.

—It's all a masquerade, my dear. And you, you enjoy it. Be my magic flute. Aren't you my accomplice, Lily?

But those men, Arik. This one with his English tea. That one with his American beer. Another with his Russian vodka. Yet another with his European wine. These cultured men who send dozens, hundreds of men, women, and children to their deaths! Who kill without setting a foot on a battlefield. Who preach peace and leave us to clean their dirty laundry! But yes, it does please me to feed them with my own hands. To be seen in their company. To play the role to the hilt in order to achieve our goal.

They look me up and down lasciviously. The unmarried ones wonder how such an ugly man landed such a luscious butterfly. The married ones envy the desire they see in your eyes.

I am not a butterfly.

My beauty is my weapon. They inhale my scent like it's a drug. This house is my web. Every object in it is bait. The decor is impeccable. The smells make their mouths water. Melted butter. *Foie gras*. Poppies. Paprika. Pecans. *Túrós Gombóc*. *Szilvás Gombóc*. Dumplings with pears. Cheese dumplings. I indulge every whim and taste. Delicacies. Curiosities. Fantasies. With my beauty, I dominate them. Disarm them. A bit of Hungarian here. Some German there. A French joke. An Italian song. Some Yiddish. Some Hebrew. Some Russian. They think like they've entered the den of a bear. Dangerous, yes, but clumsy and fat.

They are in my web!

Sometimes, listening to you from the kitchen, I laugh. Other times you make chills run up and down my spine. You threaten. Convince. Persuade. You make it all sound so inevitable. No one around the table doubts you for a second. You do as you like. They admire and hate you for that.

No time to storm the fortress. To give orders. To risk your neck. To hell with the law, with hierarchies, with fatuous egos! They support you, the cowards, even while they hope you fail. We know as much, don't we, my love? In the eyes of these mandarins and allies, so-called, you're just an attack dog. A useful tool. Nothing more.

—What does it matter, Lily! They'll always need me. And me, I don't need their love!

Your ripostes come so quickly you forget whom you're lying to, Arik. You so want their love. For them to respect and admire you. You'll do anything to hold that forbidden fruit.

War. For the sake of the Jews. For the sake of your own self-esteem.

War. For Israel. To wreak vengeance on all those who resented you in Kfar Malal. The neighbours who never voted for you. You, the only man to get out of that hellhole.

I am your shield. I watch out for your desperate need to be liked. I've seen you capitulate at the slightest display of affection. So I buttress the warrior rather than the neglected child. Nudge you towards the most invincible version of yourself. Chase away your remorse, your hesitation. Only I understand the demands war makes of you. The heartlessness. The malice. The cost. In love. In hate. In white nights.

Once the dinner guests have left, once the plans for the next attack on the enemy have been made — once night has fallen — certainty abandons you. With your nose in your files, you pace the room. Muttering to yourself. Asking my opinion about such and such. As soon as you figure I've fallen asleep, you leave.

But I'm only pretending to sleep, my love. I wait for the door to creak shut. For your departing footsteps. Then I get up to prepare for tomorrow's battle. Sycamore Farm is not Eden. It's a fortress. Forever in a state of alert, arms at the ready even on feast days.

Every night I retreat into myself. I rummage through the arsenal we've prepared in case of attacks. Crises. Scandals. Plots. Who but me, your Lily, would do this, Arik? Defend you. Support you when yours is the sole voice contradicting the rest? Surround you when they beat a retreat? Vanquish the enemy with my smile. My stratagems. I wait for you to leave the room so I can ready us for the storm.

For when friends complain about my imposing presence, or accuse me of making things worse instead of soothing your temper tantrums. When they insinuate I have too much influence, that I encourage your bullheadedness, stir up your predatory reflexes, I know I've hit the bull's eye. And if their venom poisons you, I apply the antidote. Discreetly. Do it in my own way while you contemplate the horizon.

Ah, here you are, snoring so peacefully. Does your heart have to stop before you can sleep? Sleep, *szerelmem*, sleep my love. I'll say it in my own language — in the Hungarian you find so irresistible.

Savour the quiet. Let yourself disintegrate. Return to the desert. Let your fat melt. Let hunger eat at your insides. Death is not so terrible. Who knows what will be left of you? What you'd become if you let yourself go.

I am a rock.

It's wonderful, being a rock, my love. Not to have to move anymore. Never to have to reveal what's boiling inside you. To let time, sand, air, and salt shape you. Without resisting. Without reacting. To be indifferent to the forces of erosion. To have weight. To be solid. Unshakeable. To dye myself every colour. Rust. Bronze. The grey-green of oxidized stone. And the music! The echo of dewdrops on my back.

Ploc. Ploc. Ploc.

Mineral life hums at the lower depths of death. If only you could taste it, my love . . . I'm a grain of salt on the tongue of the Earth. I dissolve in the mouths of the mountains of Sinai.

Yes, Arik, we're in one of Sinai's caves. That infernal triangle. A diamond around the neck of the Mediterranean

86

Sea. You never forget the name of this desert that so impresses and terrifies you. How often have you said to your troops over the radio: "We have entered Africa"? You, as delirious as the old explorers were, dreaming of indigo women just before the worst comes to pass.

A rout. An ambush. A miracle. A tragedy.

I'm in you like the Sinai.

I'm in your dreams, your nightmares, like the Sinai.

What moments are you searching for, my love? What pitfalls? What glory? The Mitla disaster of 1956? The catastrophe averted in 1973? What good does it do you to revive your quarrels with the desert? To revisit your retreats and advances? Are you hoping for the hurrahs of the people, the settlers, your comrades in arms? They're all alike, Arik. Scorpions under rocks. They scuttle out of their hideaways after every campaign. As jealous of your failures as they are of your success.

For you, my love, I became a rock. I crush scorpions exactly where they think they are safest. Dead or alive, I'm on guard for you. I talk to you even when you're not listening. I tell you everything, even when you're unaware of me doing so. Here in the Sinai, everything erodes except the truth.

They've wanted your hide since day one. And since the very first day they've shoved me aside. From the very first day, they've tarnished our love by shoving their religion and laws down our throats.

"Thou shalt not marry thy wife's sister, *Leviticus* 18:18!" shout the hypocritical colonizers who hug you in the streets of their settlements—yes, let's call them by their name, my love: colonizers. There's no one but you and me in this desert. Where would they be without you, tell me?

Fed and housed on the teat of the rest of the population. They multiply like rabbits while our children risk their lives in military service—obligatory except for them! Imposters wearing religious masks. Our young are posted for hours out at the checkpoints, have become executioners, gatekeepers, guard dogs, in order for their children, nestled in their flashy new houses—houses given to their parents like candy—to play in their fortresses. And then they have the nerve, these profiteers, to lecture us and vote against you any time you ask them to show a minimum of common sense.

—The longer the beard, the bigger the lie!

That's what my father used to say. He was a rabbi, but never a fool. I could have done what all the other Orthodox children did: flash my exemption card and escape military service. But I didn't. I did my part. For Israel. For that bunch of ingrates!

It wasn't the Messiah who established the first settlements by placing military camps in the heart of the conquered territories. It wasn't the Messiah who renamed them Judea and Samaria. And it was certainly not the Messiah who redrew the maps and borders under the guise of agricultural, infrastructural, and social-development projects. But so what? In their estimation, no one is pure enough.

You, too much the politician for their liking.

Me, Lily the seductress.

The one who drove her sister, Gali, to suicide and then stole her husband.

Lily the provocateur.

Who turned you against them all.

Lily guilty as charged!

She who welcomed tragedy into the house, as if Gour, my cherished nephew, all that remained of Gali, died at the age of eleven because of a curse — or, worse, to sanctify our transgressions.

You think I'm unaware, my love, of how all the slander bored into your soul? How many hours of sleep the hostile world stole from you? How every ounce of respect was drawn from your body as you defended friends and enemies? They will never be rid of you, or of me; they'll never break the bond that solders us to each other. I don't regret loving you. I've loved you since I was born, and I'll love you after I'm dead.

Before Gali, after Gali.

Before Gour, after Gour.

The wind calls me to the windows during the sleepless nights that punctuate our life at the farm. I see you leaving the stables, your long shadow beneath the moon. In the blackness I see the elongated silhouette of the young soldier in mourning.

You were my brother-in-law. But suddenly, all I could see was the man. And, for the first time, you saw me, your sister-in-law, as a woman. Two beings, two wounded souls. And between us, little Gour, like Gali's gift to us. My nephew, from then on my son. And I, his mother.

It didn't last.

Like everything else in this country, time is a mirage. Never has a land demanded so much from eternity. Never has eternity been so elusive. We have barely returned from burying Gali when life wrenches Gour from our grasp. Why such cruelty? This is the question that gnaws at you during the nights when the ghosts of Gali and Gour visit, and you console yourself by talking to the horses. This is how you hold your vigil.

He loved horses so much, our Gour did. The joy on his face when he entered the stall in Nahalal. A beautiful grey mare for his nine years! What year would that be, my love? Here in this grotto, time has neither rhythm nor form. Too bad you aren't awake. You could recite all the dates. Days. Hours. All the events. Incidents. Moments.

You have a sense of history, and of your role in that history. Events are meticulously recorded in your journal, your correspondence preserved and organized with obsessive meticulousness. Funny, isn't it, how we tend to pass over the joyous moments, while the unhappy ones are chiselled deep in our memories?

Gour is nine, so it must be...1965. Yes, that's right. You're a major-general and the director of military training. We're savouring life and, tucked away in our little apartment in the heart of the oldest moshav in the country, loving without trepidation after the loss of Gali. After years of being held back, you've finally assumed your rightful place at the head of the army. We're putting our family back together. Our attachment to each other, Gour and I, grows stronger. He's living the sort of childhood that was never available to you, loved by his friends and by us, appreciated by our moshavnik neighbours. And even though the forty deaths at Mitla still weigh on your conscience, you tell yourself: they didn't die in an ambush. You didn't sacrifice their lives in vain. They didn't die at Egyptian hands. They died for their country. And besides, more than two hundred of the enemy were felled by our machine guns. In the calculus of death, we come out ahead.

Yes... 1965... 1966... Years of deep sleep. Of contented exhaustion. Happy mornings infused with the scent of dried flowers. Running wild with the children in the nearby hills. Resting after the day's battles.

Years of victory. Conquest. This, despite occasional outbreaks of revolt and resistance. Despite the refusals to submit. Despite the stubbornness of the Palestinians.

Israel; prouder, more headstrong than ever. Neither the waste of young lives under your command in the deadly ravine of the Sinai, nor that of Arab civilians in your campaign of reprisals, keeps us awake at night.

It's before everything falls apart.

Sleep is one of those things we appreciate only when it doesn't come. When it turns its back on us. When a bullet smashes into Gour's head and our dreams expire like his breath. After 1967, there's no more night, no more peace, no more sleep. The year Israel conquers the West Bank, and the West Bank takes its revenge, white night after white night until nothing remains but the endlessly passing train of hours. Without rhythm. Without relief.

Arik, Arik? I don't hear you snoring anymore. Are you still breathing? Arik, don't leave me. Gour will not come back. He's so, so far from us now. Beyond death. With his mother, and neither you nor I can join them. Their light is an accident in our war-filled life. Their departure an accident, too.

The logic of life makes such sense when you think about it. Gali was killed on her way to Jerusalem, in the Aston Martin you gave her with the steering wheel on the right-hand side. Gour was killed by an old war trophy from the Occupied Territories, a hundred-year-old hunting rifle purchased from a West Bank villager. How can gifts be so fatal?

A breech-loading rifle that hadn't been fired since

the turn of the century. A marvellous toy as tall as the boy who's come of age in the shadow of his military father. A toy, until the morning it falls into the hands of a friend of his. Two boys playing at war, as boys do when they're the sons of soldiers.

Suddenly, the gun goes off.

A terrible scream.

An earth-shattering scream.

The bullet no one suspected was in the chamber snuffed out Gour's life as if it had been waiting for the cruellest moment to exact its revenge. You were on the telephone, I was out shopping for Rosh Hashanah... We will mourn New Year's forever.

For months the story of the rifle haunts you. To whom did it belong? Who loaded it fifty years before? A hunter? A peasant? A rebel who'd never accepted his defeat? Did whoever it was know that that bullet would kill the son of the Bulldozer of Palestine? The Butcher of Beirut? The King of Israel?

Is this the revenge of the disappeared and razed villages? Of houses reduced to dust? Of uprooted olive groves?

Is this the spiteful laughter of the natives? Have they bewitched objects? Cursed the land? Will it always be hostile, this land?

You almost go mad.

I, who never prayed, confide in anemones. I beg them to heal you each night you go out to see the horses. You ask them questions you don't dare put to me, let alone to yourself, you who are so suspicious of questions. I don't know what it is you say to the horses. You leave in a gallop, as you used to do with Gour. You disappear for hours into the rocky hills. When you come home to bed, you snuggle up against me and curl a strand of my hair around your finger. If you pull out a hair by accident, you apologize and hold me tighter. My lock of hair in hand, you rock to sleep, but sleep leaves you at sunrise two or three hours later. You leap out of bed, grateful to the new day rising and saving you from your ghosts.

And now here I am, one of those ghosts. Alone in this cave, the only one left to see you through your journey. Years pass. Vera came. Vera left. She almost managed to keep you in her forest. She almost managed to kill you, and now here I am, still here.

I'm not Vera, my love. When you looked at me it was always her I saw in your eyes. I'm not Gali, either; you sometimes looked for her in mine. Let's be honest for once. I am not the woman of your childhood, nor of your adolescence. I wasn't there at the start. I spent my youth fighting the story that preceded mine. I wasn't the first to arrive on the scene. Which may be why I didn't stay until the end. My life was an interlude. A moment of pause. A parenthesis within yours. I was dropped into a tale told by a different fairy, one who'd had you under her spell all along.

My story begins in 1947.

I'm ten years old. I'm still in Brasov, the youngest in the family. Papa's little hotel is no more, has been a sad memory for a long time. No more skiing in the Transylvanian mountains. No more tourists. Our Hungarian heritage, like our village, has been assimilated into Romania's.

As an adult I'll be accused of being cold, of lacking empathy towards the Palestinians and everything they've lost. But as a child, I'd come to know the cost of war and its aftermath.

Borders shift. One day you're part of the Hungarian Empire, and one world war later you belong to a new country. We who had always been Hungarian are suddenly Romanians! Villages change hands. People, belonging: it's a game. Those who win get to name the countries and continents.

After the Second World War, we have it figured out. We're not Hungarian and we're not Romanian. We're Jews, with a capital *J*! One after another, members of our family leave for Palestine. Now it's our turn to name the territory and take over the villages.

Cold?

Cruel?

Truth and power have this in common: they make a mockery of kindness.

In the new country, you start seeing my sister, who has joined the rest of the siblings. Gali lives in the boarding school of the Mosenson Youth Village, next to your father's field. She writes to me about her life there, and that of the other emigrants. The more she tells me, the more I'm impatient to be there with her. Among Olga, Yaffa, Eliezer, and Yitzhak, Gali is the only one who doesn't treat me like a child. She confides in me, talks about the Russian boy who waters the orange groves. She writes to me as if we were the same age. Tells me about your amorous adventures. The rendezvous among the wells. The hole you made in the school fence so she could sneak out. I imagine you, from Romania, laughing and scheming in the orchards like the canaries that sing at my window.

You're nineteen. She's sixteen, and so very beautiful. Luminous, with a childlike smile accentuated by her boyish haircut and her golden curls. You love to tangle your fingers in her hair, she tells me.

— Gali, my Gali . . . Your hair swallows me whole!

This habit you have of twirling my hair in your fingers, does it come from those first moments of love?

Gali suffers so much in your absence. During those turbulent months before the country is born you go on secret missions with the Haganah. She writes to say how much your taste for combat troubles her. The pleasure you take in reprisals against the Arabs. Your need for vengeance. And yet . . .

You were born in Palestine. In 1928, the year of your birth, Israel doesn't exist. You are Palestinian! Imagine that! To live and grow up a Palestinian Jew, like the Samaritans of Kiryat Luza, nestled in a valley on the West Bank in the shadow of Nablus. Refusing to choose between faith and nation.

Better still: living like a simple peasant.

Neither naming nor renaming yourselves.

Naming and renaming neither the land nor its people.

What am I saying? Forgive me, my dear. I've no idea where these thoughts are coming from. Ever since I've been a rock, time has passed so slowly. The water dripping on me digs little holes and then fills them with other stories, other voices. Over the years, my body has amalgamated with the earth, my veins welded to the stone. I am the loose gravel on the cave's floor. My Hungarian skin has the marly tint of clay and ancient limestone. I hear the voices of indigenous peoples.

They call us pioneers. But pioneers of what? It's in the nature of humans to believe themselves masters of their destiny. To storm across the chessboard with the presumption of queens and kings. But Vera understood and so did Gali that we were pawns in a game played by the gods. Is that what compelled my sister to become a psychiatric nurse, and then drove her to her death? If only I'd been as wise as her when I was young. I certainly was not.

I write irritated replies to Gali, and invariably end up tearing them into pieces. Her worries about you annoy me. She's loved by a young and intrepid man ready to go to war for her and she complains? She recounts your exploits but equivocates, and tempers them with reservations and shades of grey. When I read about your accomplishments, strange sensations came over me. Excitement. Envy. Melancholy. And…a delicious kind of pain. For a long time I'll feign indifference to conceal this fact: that I was in love with you before I even met you.

Gali: her sweetness, her frailty. A vulnerability that melts your heart. She awakes in you such empathy, such altruism. Only she can make you slow down, brief and ephemeral though these times are. Sometimes I hate her simply for that. Gali is the light against your darkness. She spreads innocence over the world, disarms the most recalcitrant minds with a simple hug. You're the brawler, the bad boy, the undisciplined fighter. She's the angel who attends to your wounds and soothes your loneliness.

In the months leading up to the 1948 War, the two of you are inseparable. You already envision the house you will have, the orchards you'll plant. To the great joy of your father, you want to study agronomy. Gali wants to go into nursing. Vera — surprise, surprise — is besotted with her, although you keep your relationship a secret and marry between two tours of military service without your parents' knowledge. How can your mother not approve of this young bride walking in her own footsteps? Gali is intent on a career in medicine, enough said. But Gali will never set foot in an operating theatre. She becomes a psychiatric nurse, holds the hands of the wounded, whispers comforting words into their ears. Every now and then she might change a gauze bandage. Who can compete with that?

1953, you are married.

1956, Gour is born.

In the intervening years, I too emigrate. For a time — the most beautiful but also painful period of my life — we're always together. I live nearby, look after my nephew, take my meals with you, help Gali around the house...

Oh, how handsome you are, my Arik. Handsome as your shadow at night, a shadow obscuring the ravages of age and your overeating. At thirty years old, you are exactly like the country. Lean and swaggering with the confidence and impatience of a born leader awaiting his destiny. Heedless of anyone who tries to hold you back. You've had enough of rationing and keeping an eye on the horizon. You're as twitchy as a racehorse before the gates open. Once the signal to start is given, there's no holding you back. I've seen all there is to see of man's grotesque nature. No one is a mystery to me. And you are the most handsome, most seductive open book I've come across yet.

I watch you day and night, until it hurts so much I have to hide in my apartment, get out my paints. When my brush betrays me and all that is bothering me shows up on the canvas in dark colours, I take your binoculars, the ones I pinched from your house, and go outside. Perched on a hilltop, I dream of you, wiping tears from my eyes, my only consolation the flight of birds and these binoculars you cherish pressed to my eyes as they are so often to yours. I live for these moments of escape, anything that allows me to ponder our every chance meeting, every hello or kind word from you. Tiny shocks rip through my body whenever you pay me a compliment. And if you happen to plant a kiss on my cheek, I bite the inside of my lips in order to hide my emotions.

Ah, I'm pitiful! And it kills me when anyone feels pity towards me. Who would have guessed that my devotion to you would spur such consequences? Or have we always known that it would, but never wanted to admit it? Not a day has gone by since my arrival from Romania, not a day has passed in this place I've kept secret since my childhood, without you. A place in which I am blonde, like my sister. Delicate. Innocent.

I'd rather be anything than the little brown sister. I want to be the fairy. I detest the sly fox who smiles at me from my mirror. I rail against the destiny that gave me this mouth starved of kisses and Gali such virginal lips. I turn to you like a sunflower to the sun. I desire you before I even know what the word means. My brothers used to slap my face because of my insolent expression.

Gali would mock me when she caught me looking at my reflection in the mirror. But nothing could change what I saw: that I am also beautiful. More beautiful than my sister. An untamed beauty. An indomitable beauty that makes men tremble. Nothing like Gali's porcelain loveliness.

Porcelain breaks easily. It must be kept behind glass. There to be admired. Not me! Life has tempered me, given me a harder veneer. I'm made of grass and wood. Men can do what they like with me, to me. It infuriates me that you should succumb, like so many others, to this fragility to be adored from a distance and handled with care. Go ahead, love my sister. Fail to see what to me is as clear as day. That you're too strong for her, Arik, and she's too weak for you.

I want you to sculpt me with your hands. Burn me. Shape me. Fashion a cauldron out of me. Bathe yourself in me! I long for the day when the porcelain breaks. She will break. Sooner or later you'll realize the mistake you've made.

The country is never not at war. The militias have been organized into a formidable army. Recruits are sought everywhere. When it comes to killing, men and women are equally welcome. I respond to the call to arms. I work as a police artist, for the department of judiciary identity before it's integrated into the information sector.

Did it ever occur to me that I might be assigned to

your brigade? Maybe yes, maybe no. The line between wishing and planning is such a fine one. Gali never wanted me to pursue a military path and neither did our parents. When she hears of my intention to join, she bombards me with long speeches about the gift I'm squandering. She who insists I study art. Who encourages me to take courses in interior design and even ornithology.

—You're too beautiful and you love beauty too much to go to war, she cries. You love music and museums and nature too much!

Is she talking about me or her? Is she reproaching me for my love of beauty or is she envious of it? She spends her days among people broken by mental illness, helping unfortunate men and women let down by nature. It feels as if Gali hates it that I'm ignoring the splendour that surrounds me. Is she jealous of the time I'll be spending with you, participating in the thing beyond agriculture that you care about most—combat? I would be, if I were her...

All I recall now is an immense happiness, the feeling of my heart enveloping the whole of me, the conviction that, unlike the other paratroopers under your command, were I ever to jump from a plane I'd float up to the stars. Finally, I have you all to myself. The army belongs to us alone, the army in which you finally discover the affection your parents never provided you. From that time forward, I am a part of its great embrace.

The idea that we might find warmth and comfort among sanctioned murderers repulses my sister. But what does she know, after all? Before love, hatred unites people against one another. Put a gun in women's or men's hands and they are equals under the canopy of death.

What does she know of the sweet satisfaction of violence after imagining all the ways your enemy might be put to death, the taste of his blood? What does she know of the irresistible appeal of weaponry? Tanks call out to you. Summon you into their bellies, to deliver them of their bombs. Machine guns seize you at night. Cold. Trembling. Beg you to rid them of their cartridges. To give them life. To let fire flow from their mouths. Once you hold the means of death in your hands, nothing in the world matters except the desire to deploy it. To throw a grenade as far as possible and harvest souls.

I enter your world as though I was always made for it. I penetrate where Gali cannot follow. There where the planting of clementine trees and land mines is not a contradiction. Not a conflict. Joining the information sector places me in your shadow realms. Another kind of intimacy. I no longer know where state secrets end and those of the heart begin.

At first you're wary, even brutal. Your tone is more severe with me than it is with the other soldiers. But once we're alone, your attitude changes so swiftly I'm flabbergasted. A guileless warrior, you've never been a very good actor.

Ah! Uri's little ministrations—how it flummoxes you when the young journalist, a bit too cockily, looks me up and down when we're in headquarters. I swear, my love, it occurs to me from time to time to encourage him, if only to get a rise out of you. The other soldiers are quick to warn him off:

—Uri, you're better off staying away from the commander's sister-in-law!

But it works the other way, doesn't it? He steals you from me. I must be satisfied sharing you with Uri and the entire country. Poor Uri. Your stroke ends up killing him. Dead less than a year after you went into a coma—as happens with old married couples.

On the military base we believe we're being so discreet, you and I. We're blind to the bemused expressions of the other brigadiers. Deaf to their whispers. Out of respect for you they stick their heads in the sand, when truly the whole world knows about our love even before we know it ourselves. For several months, we avoid the inevitable. But the inevitable always arrives.

The desert.

The war.

The disaster.

It's no coincidence, my Arik, that we find ourselves in this cave in the Sinai, surrounded by these mountains.

How often has the Sinai almost taken you from me? And yet, without the catastrophe of Mitla Pass, where would we be today?

1956. A sad year even before the fatal day of October 31. The doctors inform you and Gali that you will never be parents. I begin to imagine us together. I even imagine Gali asking you for a separation. It's in her nature to sacrifice herself. Who am I to stop her from being who she is? I see us marching on—you, eventually Commander-in-Chief and the Minister of Defence, why not? And me slowly rising up the ranks of the information sector.

After three years of marriage, Gali's belly begins to swell. The whole castle-in-the-air crumbles in a pile of dust. If it weren't for my birds and my art, I'd go insane. At night I listen to Mozart to hide my distress. Just before dawn, in the hour before I have to leave for headquarters at Tel-Nof, I watch the starlings for an hour with the binoculars I stole from you. The Suez War heats up. The British set a trap for the Egyptians and we are the bait. I'm not afraid of the beginning of the attack, but of how it will end. It's the war of last chance. I make sure I'm responsible for the index-ing and organizing of the photographs transmitted by our scouts and spies on the ground. For you, my commander, my oxygen, my reason for being, I would pick every flea in the desert. Are we not accomplices? Two soldiers in the same fight? Are we not facing in the same direction together? You don't have to explain or justify a thing to me.

Death is death. War is war.

If we want to win, we have to sink our teeth into the task.

If we want the land, we have to tear up the fruit trees along with the weeds.

Lions eat their young.

Wild boars trample everything in their way.

Only the strong survive.

She detests this view of the world, Gali does. She obstinately sets about finding reason in the lives of her psychiatric patients. She believes in the Utopian discourse of our Zionist forebearers. Refuses to consider what must be done in the name of this Utopia. Refuses to recognize her role and responsibility in its realization. Is it that she understands, in the end, but lacks the courage to go on? And am I awful for thinking that?

The war, like her death, makes us closer. I'm ready to kill every Arab in the world to be by your side. I would follow you, my love, to the Gates of Hell. To the Gates of Hell, I follow.

I can hear you snoring. Good, darling. Sleep. Some things we can only accept under anaesthetic. Quick. Eager. Impatient. That's what you are when confronted by your anguish. The very idea of anguish unnerves you.

— Anguish is a luxury, you keep repeating, endlessly.

I say "you," but to be honest, I'm the same. I have

to become ill for us to slow down and face our fears. When the doctor uses the word "cancer," you frown at him as if he's some sort of traitor. You don't even let him finish his diagnosis. What kind of cancer, you ask? Where's the tumour? Its progression? What's the prognosis? Hopeful? Hopeless? Uncertain? None of that concerns you.

It's winter, 1999. An unusually cold February. The final year of the millennium is barely underway. The idea I won't be there to mark the year 2000 is, for you, simply unthinkable. The doctor's explanations roll off you like water off a raincoat. You want a solution: this is how we're going to proceed. You want the only words that matter: lung cancer is nothing to be concerned about; all we have to do is —

But the words you yearn for don't come. The doctor, fearing the wrath of the most rancorous man in Israel, recommends a specialist in New York. We leave for the United States like those dreamers of a former age embarking for the New World. There, where life can start afresh and miracles fall from the sky.

During the entire the trip you rail against the educated Jews of the day who've not lived the miracle of Israel. Doctors rendered complacent by their comfortable lives. No longer even trying to make the effort. They don't believe in the impossible, but content themselves with the way things are! You make a list of initiatives for the new Israeli millennium.

— This will be priority number one for the Knesset! you declare.

A whole suite of remedies for the laxity that drives you crazy. The apathy and self-satisfaction of the victors who destroy empires. The resignation that turns something as banal as lung cancer into an insurmountable obstacle.

When the American oncologist repeats the same diagnosis, and advises us — with a sort of empathetic expression verging on pity — that we should continue treatment in Israel, you remain silent. At a loss for words. At a loss for everything, even anger. Ariel Sharon has finally met his match.

I've known for a long time that I will die of cancer. Before we even land in New York, my love, I know that soon I'll be leaving you. But I don't have the courage to tell you. The idea that I will die before you brings me comfort. Not to have to attend your funeral. To have to live alone, like your mother. To have to remake myself without you. To wonder who I am, who I might have been had I not loved you.

I'll no longer have to fight against Gali's and Gour's ghosts. Or Uri's friendship, and the confidences you share as two comrades in arms. Or against all the young soldiers who idolize you. Or my own jealousy of all who love you.

I'm even jealous of those who hate you! What is hatred but another kind of love? I'm jealous of your certainties: that only the present and future matter. That to cultivate the land is to vanquish it. That whatever is deracinated must have needed to be torn up. That there's nothing to regret.

On New Year's Eve, our house at Sycamore Farm catches fire. It's a sign: one month, two months, three months? Like the century, I will expire.

All my life, I've been living on time borrowed — from my sister, from my nephew, from the soldiers who have died under your command. From the nameless peasants struck from history. Is this the fate of all women: to turn around and contemplate the horror in the wake of men's march towards history?

During my last days in the hospital, your worried look weighs upon my swollen eyelids. That piercing gaze that refuses to shift for fear that death will take it by surprise. Life is draining from me, and you scold me.

— You must fight, Lily. Fight! Fight! What is lung cancer to you? You've survived much worse! We've nurtured a country, you and I. That fool of an American said you wouldn't live to see the new century. Well, here we are! It's March already, Lily. March, 2000. Don't you see? This is no time to give up! When have you ever surrendered to the enemy? Tell me!

You become furious whenever I bring up my imminent death. You refuse to listen to my wishes — snapping back at me, before I even finish my sentence:

— When you're well, you can do all that yourself.

I didn't get well, my love. I died like any other woman. You planted anemones on my grave at the top of our hill on Sycamore Farm.

I've been snuggling up to death for ten years. And I'm waiting. Here in this red cave, rocky, crystalline. I'm waiting for you to finally let yourself go so that we can be together again. In the land of the living it's 2010. You've been asleep for four years, Arik. I'm tired of waiting. I've begged the woman-voice to bring you home to me.

—Rare are the ones who survive the stream of their conscience, she warns me.

What if you liberated yourself from your body, Arik? What if you gave yourself willingly to nothingness? If you broke free from the land of men. Their wars. Their desires. Their violence? If you dared to plunge into the Gehenna of women. Then would you come back to me?

For you, I've cut off a lock of my hair. For you, I offered the woman-voice my body. For you, I became a rock in this cave. The limestone water washes over and shapes me. Four years since your stroke. I'm no longer the same as I was. Not that it matters, she kept her promise.

I know you're terrified. Weak. Naked. Forsaken. A slave of your body. Without the binoculars you use to spot the enemy at night. I know you're terrified, my love. I was too. I still am, a bit... Forgive me, my darling, for tearing you away from yourself.

So that I could see you again, I made a pact with the ghosts. I entrusted my memory, and the memories of all women, to the woman-voice. And so that you'd listen to me, I gave her my voice and the voice of every woman. So that you'd be able to rest near these stones, I gave her my soul. I had so much more to tell you. Cancer carried me away. If I tell you my secrets, will you stay here with me? Or forge your own road? Would you leave me here in this cave to erode into the Sinai?

Whatever you decide is not important, my love. Know that I will always love you.

Now wake up, my Arik.

Wake up.

ARIK

Something is tickling his cheek. Has he collapsed at the feet of death? Is it death caressing him like this? Arik strains his eyelids. Forms take shape in the darkness. Familiar features. Parts of faces. Dark hair tied up in a chignon. Pronounced eyebrows. Oval chin. Nose protruding over luscious lips. An intense gaze concealed by oversized sunglasses à la Brigitte Bardot.

Lily!

Is he dreaming? Is it her hand brushing his face? A strand of her hair? He must absolutely not open his eyes. Lily might slip between his eyelids. He wouldn't be able to feel her sweetness on his cheek anymore. Or press his body against hers—he knows now, he's certain—the warm body sleeping close beside him is his wife's. A body so desired, so loved. He'll look and see. And if Lily isn't there, he'll be alone in the semi-darkness. The prickling on his cheek will have been no more than the wind. Or worse, his own breath. And that would be the end. Once you look, it's impossible to imagine anything other than what you see before you.

Eyesight is murderous. It kills remorselessly. It turns a human being into a predator. Twin orbs level in the middle of the face, synchronized for a better fix on the prey trapped even before it's caught. When we fix our gaze, everything that isn't the target disappears. *Tunnel vision*, the English call it. The rest of the world clouds over. There are only two beings on Earth: the eater and the eaten.

Arik always keeps his eyes open. He's a lion. A tiger. A hyena. Irises in the same place, focused on the same object. One and the same face. His own. Wolves. Condors. Eyesight kills. He learns this truth on the day he peers through a pair of night-vision binoculars for the first time and sees red silhouettes stumbling about in the darkness, unaware of the danger. He observes them the entire night, his enemies' position given away by the heat of their bodies, glowing like embers in the night. One signal from him and his soldiers would mow them down. He feels, in the moment, a surge of utter satisfaction, and subsequently he never goes anywhere without his binoculars. Never closes his eyes again. When the vision of one eye is impaired due to a detached retina, he does everything he can to hide the fact. For fear of letting himself be caught unawares. Of being surprised by a hunter with sharper eyesight than his.

A predator. The child of a predatory country. He makes this his vocation. Beauty. Life. Music. Smells. Tastes. Rocky hills and smooth plains: these are all dangerous seductions. Comforts proffered to cattle before the abattoir.

1952. As a young commander, Arik sets up an ambush against the Jordanians. Between the 1948 war that made Israel a reality and the war of 1967 that made of it a hegemonic power with its own colonies and colonial subjects, the country's borders are porous. Uprooted, the Palestinians mount a resistance from neighbouring countries worried about the insatiable appetite of the new state hungry for conquest. Whether out of pity, guilt, or political strategy, they let the Palestinians carry on.

Arik secretly envies the Palestinians who infiltrate the border *kibbutzim*. And the more he envies them, the greater his need to destroy them. Their resistance spreads. Their incursions, of little consequence at first — cattle and donkeys stolen from the settlers — intensify. Sabotage. Arson. Ambushes that are occasionally fatal. Obstinate in defeat, they sow confusion and fear all along the borders. They are like irritating insects, repeatedly swatted but refusing to die. Insects that leave no one in peace. They ruin evenings on the verandah, that portion of the territory thought to have been tamed, cleared of wild fauna and flora, of all those persistent indigenous plants that spoil a well-kept lawn. These insects belong to the night — and the night, like the territory, belongs to them.

Arik understands this from the very start — that he has to master the terrain and incorporate it if he is to rid its indigenous elements of their indigeneity. Pull the rug out from beneath their feet. Chew up the land centimetre by centimetre. Erase their native footprints. But how he envies them their damned indigeneity! Their gift for being one with the land. He envies the audacity it inspires. The sense of belonging. Of inalienable attachment. These peasants transformed from one day to the next into guerilla fighters and revolutionaries. He even envies them their reputation as terrorists. The legend of them. Their myth of them. *Them.* So small. So vulnerable! He would like to be a terrorist himself. To taste this audacity that only the vanquished know.

However, on this day in 1952, he must content himself with taking on the Jordanians. An enemy of the second tier, a prey that leaves his hunger unassuaged. Whatever. He'll make use of them to hone his hunter's instincts. He heads towards the Jordan River, near a dilapidated bridge, sees a tiny Jordanian police station on the other bank, and a few figures in the shadows. Putting his weapon down, he signals to them from a distance, requesting a meeting. Mollifying his aquiline features as much as he is able, his back stooped, he feeds them a tale of cattle stolen from the Ma'oz Chaim kibbutz. He asks for their help, the sort of co-operation between adversaries over a mundane matter that allows each to recover a bit of humanity and civilized behaviour. A way of saying: look, I'm not an animal. I did not choose to fight a war. I'm just obeying the orders of my superiors.

In the moment, standing together amid the ruins of the bridge, the two sides are no more than neighbours sharing the same river. So convincing is Arik that the Jordanian policemen, themselves peasants before joining the army, are immediately sympathetic. Arik licks his lips, like a fisherman alerted by a pull on the net. It's too good an opportunity, the ruse is ridiculously easy. The fish is coming to him.

Under the pretext of discussing the problem of vandalism and theft along the border, he brings them to the Israeli side where they can exchange pleasantries and discuss strategies in the shade of a large acacia tree. For a moment, they are no longer enemies. The tension in their bodies relaxes, the suspicion in their demeanour abates. Their formerly curt and careful replies become more and more expansive. Their conversation is agreeable, almost convivial. They share what they have to drink and, peasant to peasant, give each other tips on the best way to raise cattle.

They're appealing, these policemen. Arik feels bad lying to them. His lapse worries him, and he lowers his antennae. The ones that sense how refreshing drinks are when shared by chance companions. The ones that amplify the outbreak of shared laughter. The ones that pick up the common odour of men's sweat. That absorb the moist warmth of a reassuring palm on the shoulder, of a hand shaken as a sign of friendship. Anything that stirs the slightest suggestion of compassion, he annihilates.

Predator. He needs a clear view and two quarries offer themselves up to his line of sight. Two precious pieces in a game of power he's determined to win. They'll be useful as ransom to obtain the release of Israeli soldiers who, a few weeks back, made the mistake of infiltrating territory under Jordanian control and getting caught. Thanks to the overconfidence of the police officers—thanks to his own mendacity—he would prove himself as a military commando. No one would question his hunter's instincts anymore.

On that day, another reality was revealed to him. Seeing kills. Kills hearing. Kills touching. Kills smell. Kills taste. A clear view would be his weapon and his compass. One after another, Arik deletes his childhood reminiscences. Of cool naps on hot afternoons. Siestas in the shade of the wagon after ploughing. The comforting taste of his mother's cooking.

He is a predator. Predators don't shut their eyes. They don't hear the calls of starlings. They don't count butterflies. They experience no delight in the buzzing of bees among flowers. Predators seek neither love nor friendship, neither humanity nor civility. Predators confiscate these indulgences, offerings to gods and emperors.

As a teenager, he is hurt by his mother Vera's coldness, and the detestation of his neighbours. But as an adult, he laughs at such things. Follies that deserve nothing but scorn. The grief of the vanquished has no place in history. Arik is a conqueror, was born to *write* history. After the binoculars are in his hands, after the trick he played on the Jordanian border is successful, after the astonished silence of the Jordanian policemen confronted with his rifle is forgotten, after he has uprooted the acacia tree and those who met under it, everything that unsettles him is silenced, and the bright colour of the sun is no more than a spotlight shining down upon the enemy, facilitating his tearing them to pieces.

Sight is an assassin. The master of assassins. Sight seizes on a body like a marauder. Deprives it of all other senses. Of its dimensions. Makes of it nothing but paper. Makes the world flat. Makes it a map, to be folded and unfolded. Redrawn to please the eye. Spoils. A simple X marking the spot of the next conquest.

Arik keeps his eyes open, always has. The entire world is territory to be bulldozed. Houses nothing but facades. With no interiors, no inhabitants. Models to be destroyed. And why not? Raptors do not question their predatory nature. Aged fifteen, the day he joined the ranks of the Haganah militia, he made his decision: he would be the most accomplished bird of prey!

His eyes are always open, except —

Except when it comes to Lily. Lily and her hair. Lily and her laugh. Lily and her unequivocal gaze. Who would abandon him only once, on the day of her death. Lily who has come to his aid in his hour of need, when he's perched on death's doorstep, drowning, killed by his mother, and relentlessly hounded by the voice of the woman-sorceress. Only Lily knows how to calm the voracious monster in him. She consoles him after the loss of his loved ones, though she too is in mourning for her sister and nephew.

Lily. Sister-in-law. Aunt. Mother. Lover. Wife. Accomplice. Lioness among lions.

He's obese. She loves him. He rages. She loves him. He's an assassin. She loves him anyway. Only with Lily does he close his eyes. As he does now.

Something is tickling his cheek. No! Not just anything. The only thing possible: a strand of his wife's black, lustrous mane burying her neck as she lies beside him. He who loves maps so, traces the country's geography with Lily's long tresses, black rivers on white sheets, planting kisses here and there to mark the cardinal points, cities, regions.

These unruly curls on her forehead: the Sea of Galilee.

The wavy strands on her right temple: the Dead Sea.

The tender teasing of her hair on his cheek … beckoning him to play.

Guess where I'm from, Arik. From the north? Where it rains on my roots, and shows how white they are? Where the colour fades until my next visit to the hairdresser? Am I from the temples? From the slopes of Mount Carmel facing the sea? There, where the land breaks up into stone terraces, one over another, like the pangs of love? Am I the Galilee of women? Their crown, their Nazareth, a citadel perched at the highest point of their most secret desires? There, where their furrowed brows shine under a sea of silky hair, washed, combed, tied up and gathered up into a small chignon, as if the rebellious hair of the world was striving to rekindle their shattered childhoods and return them to the cradle?

And if I came from the backcountry of women's tresses? The place where, when they're tired, they let their weary heads fall back on the worn headrest of their divan, or against the sticky tiles of the bathroom, or the wardrobe door, or the mirror they don't dare look at anymore? That place where ringlets that used to fly in the morning breeze are crushed under the weight of their worries, their migraines, their heads bent over the sink or raised to the dirty ceiling to let the sweat run away from their eyes? Tell me, where do I come from?

From the south! Arik wants to answer. From the nape of my Lily's neck. From the Negev of her hair, the anemones of Sycamore. From the farm.

The words don't leave his lips. He can't feel his tongue. His mouth won't open. Powerless, he waits for her hair to answer. For its reassuring smile. For it to tell him: yes, I am from the south. We'll find each other there soon. You'll wake up and roll me between your fingers as you lie in bed with Lily.

Arik waits and waits.

From the south?

The words cut through the silence.

What south, Arik? What do you know about a woman's shallows, her founts, her hollows? Yes, I come from the south. I tumbled down from the scorched locks of Beersheba, my ends so dry they ripped the teeth from the combs.

I am the surviving hair of the women and children of Qibya, crammed in the houses levelled with explosives under your command. Too afraid to move, or to say a word, they die huddled together as a single corpse while your soldiers watch the flames.

I come from the Dead Sea of women-salt. Women-dust. I come from the earth sucked dry of water. Of its lifeblood. Of its sap. Sucked dry by invasive fruit trees. Industrial trees laden with chemicals. Trees that exhaust the underground aquifers, that inject themselves into the open veins of hills and rivers. That disperse their transgenic seed throughout the indigenous basin. That bear monstrous fruit to nourish monstrous men.

Tropical fruit in an arid climate, their thirst never

quenched. The gluttonous harvest of visionary settlers. Who plant their settlements like they do avocados. Gluttonous fruit for gluttonous men.

Avocado-men. Belly-mouth-men. Gut-monsters. They suck the earth's breasts until they are nothing but wrinkled skin. Putrified. Drained of their juice. Their milk. Their honey. They gobble up the land. Chew its ribs one by one. Slice. Grind. Crush the soil.

There, where the avocado trees carpet the valleys, fields of wheat and barley and sesame used to stretch as far as the eye could see. Their stems were golden hair against the blue sky. I come from these fields that once nourished whole villages. I am the daughter of the grain you trucked to market when you wanted tools and furniture. That women bartered for silk to embroider. For shawls. Woven baskets. Clay pots.

I am all that's left of the clouds that shrouded the watermelons after a long summer's day. My hair that once danced in the wind has been pulled out. The manes of my mares that used to knead the land with their hooves and spread the pollen of cypress trees with their tails have been cut off.

I am the one who ran during the time of white horses. I'm all that remains of the ravaged earth. Violated. Ancestral tenderness mowed down. Humiliation after humiliation.

I am not a lock of hair.

I'm the story no one tells.

The voice you have shut up inside yourself.

The woman-voice.

The river spat you out. The desert took you in. Time passes. Stops. The time of water. The time of rock. Here is your life. Your death. Your ailing body.

I tend to you. I plug the hole made by your mother's bullet. I cover you with my hair. With all I have left of my dignity. If only I, too, could be a predator, Arik. Take pride in my vision. Devour you with a look. Sweep over every inch of your repugnant body. Sink my teeth into your mass of flaccid skin. Scrape you from this land!

Arik jolts up.

He opens his eyes. Everything is dark. He feels his face, his eyelids, touches the whites of his eyes. Yes, they're open. He rubs them. Nothing works. He can't speak! He can't see! Where is he? Where's Lily? Gilad? Uri? Is he in the hospital? In his bed? In hell? Is this a dream? A nightmare?

A current of air raises the hair on his neck, thighs, stomach, groin. His penis! His belly quivers in the wind. He's naked. Naked! Oh, the thought of being seen like this — his drooping belly exposed to his enemies, his chin drooling down his neck, the false folds of flesh dangling down both sides of his body. Over the cheeks of his ass. Over his penis and scrotum. That someone might see him in this state. Defenceless. Without eyes. Without his weapon. His compass. The idea is insupportable.

He waves his arms, sweeps them wildly over his body. He's too massive, can't hide his nakedness. He's alone. Alone. Alone in the dark.

—Arik...

That voice.

—Arik.

She's everywhere. Here. Down there. Up there.

She rises up from the very ground. From the rock. From all sides.

The voice is coming from him. From deep inside him. Tormenting him. Like a dagger.

—Arik! Arik! Arik!

Every time he hears his name he wants to throw up. His body convulses. Nausea overwhelms him. Rises up in his throat. Fills his mouth. Swamps his parched lips. He clasps his hands over his mouth. The torrent is too strong. Vomit spurts through his nose, his ears, his eyes. Between the fingers he has clamped to his lips. Runs in thick gobbets down his chin, his neck, onto his chest, over his breasts.

—Leave yourself behind, Arik. Flush your cadavers out.

He wants to cry out: NO.

He's pinned in place by a second surge of bile.

—Your body no longer belongs to you, Arik. It hasn't for a long time. Leave it to its raging.

No. This body has protected him. Occupied all his space. Colonized the air around him. Forced open doors for him. This gargantuan body. Confident. Striving. Greedy for everything. Food. Life. Power. Land. Water. Trees. Sky. Wind. This body would not betray him.

Arik searches the void, looking for Lily, for her face. He calls out. Is answered by a gurgling in his stomach. The sharp burn of acid reflux rising from his stomach to his throat.

His body shouts: free me, deliver me from this torture.

Suddenly a tepid flow of liquid mixed with some more sticky substance. The stench of urine and feces. His legs move slowly, then collapse under him. As if they no long remember how to walk. As though he's lost his limbs and is nothing but a formless mass of flesh.

He crawls on all fours, fighting with all his strength the urge to throw up. One hand feeling the ground, the other held out ahead of him. An arm is placed gently but firmly under his armpit. He bites at it like a wild dog, and scampers away, scuttles towards a warmth, a distant glimmer of light at the end of the darkness. He flees, flees, leaving a trail of piss behind him. If he keeps going, will he tumble over a cliff? Will he get out of this hell?

Too late. The arm grabs him by the neck. He bats at it trying to save himself, struggles against the weight of his traitorous body. Lily! Where is Lily? Why has she left him?

—Get up, Arik. It's Lily you want? I'm Lily.

Startled, he lowers his guard.

—Lean on my arm. I'm taking you to the source.

Step by step, the voice guides him towards the light, a thin arm supporting the wounded, declawed animal. A solid, stable arm. Was it Lily who tickled his cheek? Was hers the acid voice that demolished his citadel stone by stone? To the source, it said. Deep down, Arik knows it's not Lily. Lily would never have let him suffer like this. And if it actually was her? What if, as he has always feared, every love in his life had been nothing but an illusion? An offering to the predator? What if here—at this moment, in this dark, discombobulating place, Lily was finally telling the truth? Does she love him? Hate him? Did she ever love him? What if she was this woman who is torturing him, this honey-voiced demon? Then why, suddenly, is she being so kind to him?

So many questions, he has. He who never attributed any value to questions, never knew doubt, or tolerated uncertainty, or had anything to do with dilemmas. Questions get in the way. Dilemmas are superfluous. Doubts? A waste of time and energy. He has only contempt for such pitiful souls, racked by uncertainty and hesitation. Wretched people who squander their lives in the contemplation of choices, carefully weighing the pros and cons of actions that have no repercussions except on their own miserable good consciences. Souls who approach life as philosophers do in their quest for eternal verities. Answers are comforting to them, especially answers that lead to more questions.

Well, this country was not founded on questions! It wouldn't exist at all if the Zionists had anguished over the legitimacy of their cause, of their right to appropriate land; had they asked permission to settle on the hilltops and cover their flanks with exotic orchards. This country was founded on answers. Solutions. Audacious, egregious behaviour.

Seventy years of solutions.

Questions are dangerous. They introduce nuance. They cause consternation, fatal in wartime. And what is the world but a vast battlefield? Questions halt the march of history. Sirens, when they sing, distract troops, make them waver, drill holes of reticence in their clear tidy orders. Before his comrades can stop him, a sensitive soldier turns his back on the enemy, just for a second, just long enough for him to listen to his conscience, and POW! Another corpse on the ground. Even so, for the first time, Ariel Sharon is unsure. Slips and slides into this intolerable greyness.

Who is he? Who is she? Who's speaking to him? What is this carnivorous body he's been lugging around for decades, this *rapacious* body? What has he been gorging on and shitting all these years, if not answers and solutions? Efficacious answers. Workable ones. Thanks to force of arms. Answers and solutions that don't anticipate or instigate questions. So busy taking pride in his conquests, he's never asked himself if a solution just might be that, if an answer really answers anything.

How many victims for each victory? He has consumed so many, his body is regurgitating them, and here he is: emptied, his body used. Like a garbage bag.

— Look out for the rock, his companion whispers. Lift your leg, Arik.

He obeys, happy for once to obey a voice other than his own. What a strange feeling this docility is.

— A bit to the right.

Beneath his feet the mud turns to solid earth, the earth to sand, sand to dunes. The dunes dance, crumble in gusts, and the gusts shift, become entangled in the fronds of palm trees, the palm trees drop their dates, the dates fall noiselessly to the ground, their echoes stifled. The hard earth softens.

Arik, sightless, stretches out his hand, feels his surroundings. A carpet of flowers, petals outstretched, their sex open to the day and at the end of his fingertips. He recognizes the velvety texture of anemones, Lily's favourite flower. Is he going to her tomb? He whom Death terrified, now welcomes it. Would willingly take shelter in its arms.

How many years has he been in a coma? How many years in this body? How many years has he endured this torture? Death. Yes, Death, take me. Save me from this nightmare. He quickens his step. His guide's arm holds him back.

—No, Arik. You're not going to die. Not yet. Here, time does not run out. It moves in circles, waves, spirals.

They move forward, the dense warmth dissipated from time to time by a fresh breeze that reminds him he's naked, stirs up the reek of vomit and urine. If only he could find a hole and hide in it. He's naked, he's blind, at the mercy of this woman-voice, this hair-woman pretending to be Lily. He so wishes she were. That she would rescue him from his impotence. Impotence compounded by shame. By the salutary kindness of this voice. His legs quake. The arm holds him more tightly.

—A little farther, Arik. The source is very near.

He hears birds, running water, the steps of animals come to quench their thirst. He recognizes the sound of oryx rubbing their horns against the stiff water plants. Is she bringing him to an oasis?

—I'm bringing you back to life, Arik. To memory. To time. Here. We've arrived.

She leads him to a rock. The surface is smooth, soft under his flayed buttocks. A rock imbued with heat. She sits him down by the water.

—Go on. Soak your feet.

The water is hot. A velvety steam envelops him. The voice supports him as he gently lowers himself. His feet, then his knees. After his knees, his thighs. After his thighs, his penis, stomach, his torso, one arm, then the other. The underground stream breaks up against his dark mass, goes around it, reassembles. He is a tear in the fabric. An intrusion. A parasitical element disturbing the flow of ... of what?

His story? Memory? Life? All his mistakes and the atrocities he has committed? And what about his loves? His passions? His successes? His victories? His glory? Is he not a hero?

Uri Dan told him he was. He's the King of Israel.

Lily told him he was. He's the best of them all.

Isn't he the nation's saviour? Where have all his certainties gone?

—Go ahead. Dive in.

After his arms, his shoulders. After his shoulders, his neck, his chin, his mouth, his nose. Bubbles of air rise up around him. Burst against his closed eyelids. His hair rises and floats in the water. No more tentacles. No more maelstrom. No more monsters. He is light. So light! He wants to encrust himself with pebbles from the source's hollow.

The woman-voice's arm is back under his armpit, pulls him up.

He's cold.

—Don't worry, you'll warm up.

Steered back to the rock, he shrinks, gathers his legs up to cover his nakedness.

A roguish laugh. So like Lily's!

—Don't bother, Arik. In my eyes, you'll always be naked.

Lips on his lips. A silken bubble slides from the tongue of the stranger down his throat.

—I've had your voice in me for a long time. Now I'm giving it back to you. Tell me whatever you want. Ask me all the questions. Judge me, if you wish. Kill me if you must. I am yours. I've always been yours.

—You're not Lily.

He's surprised to hear his own voice. That he is articulating words after so many years of silence.

—I am Lily, just as I am Vera. And so many other women inside you. When I am no one, I am simply . . . Rita.

—I've known a lot of Ritas!

Within the hoarse grain of his voice are traces of the man he was.

—None like me.

—Tell me who you are. Deliver me!

—The beginning of my story is the end of yours. Are you ready to die, Arik?

—We all have to die.

—Then let us die. Here is my story.

RITA

I was born the day of my death. A tiny blue cadaver in the arms of Houriyya, the midwife.

— Houriyya is an Arabic name.

— Yes, it's an Arabic name.

— Are you Arabic?

— What about you, Arik? Are you Jewish?

— Stupid question!

— What does it mean to be Jewish?

— To suffer.

— Have you suffered?

— I'm suffering now!

— And what does it mean to be an Arab in this country?

— I don't know what it means to be an Arab! What does it mean to be on the losing side? Let them tell you how they feel in this country.

Houriyya felt life. In her hands, babies who should

never be alive are born. Me, I fell out of my mother's womb, dead. Everyone but Houriyya gave up on me. Hourriya massaged my belly. Whispered to me in Arabic. Pinched my bottom. Kissed my blue lips. Suddenly, a nightingale crashed against the window. I opened my mouth and screamed.

—She's alive! My grandmother cried.

Houriyya went outside without saying a word. She picked up the dead bird lying in the grass and put it in my cradle.

—Little nightingale. You'll soar high, very high, until the day when you fall again. Other deaths will come. Other lives, too. You will follow the river to its source, traverse plains, climb hills, chant your name like a call to exiles. You will *be*. Bird. Horse. Poem. Death will never again leave you. You are the stillborn child of a stillborn land.

My mother breaks into tears. My father falls on his knees and prays. My grandmother grabs me and chases the midwife from the house. So I might live, Houriyya has exhausted her every miracle. Since her death, I wander among the dead. I wear all the faces. The faces of those this country kills and rears. One day, I too will use up all the miracles. Only Houriyya will recognize me. I am Rita. The woman-voice. The woman-nightingale. The stillborn child of a stillborn land.

—Stop saying those words! Every birth is violent. For this country to be born, others have to die.

—So come.

—Where are you taking me?

—To my birth. To my violence.

Don't frown, Arik. Like you, I come of age in a house of settlers. Like you, my brothers work in the fields and the orchards, and I with the cattle and the goats. Like you, they put a knife in my hand whenever we go to the market, where Arabs and Jews intermingle. Like you, I believe olive trees grow on our side of the fence. But then one day I come across olive trees moving along the dusty road that runs down our portion of the moshav. A forest of olive trees, hovering above the ground. Their roots like a thousand feet—a thousand long, thread-like toes. They swarm in unison, barely touching the soil. A *corps de ballet* in synchronicity. Branches waving in the air. Where are they going? There, where the ballerinas will be in shadow? On the stage behind the curtain? In the dark? The olive trees hover. Their felty leaves twirl and pepper the road. They mix in with the villagers on the military trucks. Shoes and shawls are strewn along the road with the leaves and crushed olives. Time passes. The uprooted trees disappear, and then—

—It appears.

—What appears, Arik?

—The forest. Right at the edge of our moshav. A forest of olive trees. As if it had always been there. Ha!

—Why are you laughing?

—Why not? Trees that move by themselves? That can be torn out of the ground without dying? That travel from one end of the country to the other? It's ingenious! These uprooted olive trees taught me something critical: anything can be moved, even trees. If anything can move, everything is possible. I could change the axis of the Earth if I wanted to!

—Then you could make the olive trees lie, if you wanted to.

—What do you know about it? Everything in this country moves. Men. Women. Villages. Roads. Houses. Borders. Names. Even the centuries. Savvy is the man who can predict the direction of the wind. Me, I've learned how to do so. I've learned how to move borders. Reorient the roads. Have them go where I tell them to go. Until no highway, no exit, no shortcut does not lead to Israel. East. West. North. South. Gaze skyward. Plunge into the heart of the country. Everything belongs to me. History and the ruins of history dance to my beat!

Everything moves. And nothing moves. Not life. Not death. Those who are born are already dead. Those who die have never been alive. Everything is moving, disappearing.

So we dig. We sink our shovels into the flesh of ancient villages. We strip temples and empty mines. Dump the pottery shards into a museum somewhere. Dig ourselves a history. Excavate a great black hole, a junk-room where we place our lies. Let them ferment. Make miracles of them. Get drunk on miracles. Spew up miracles to make a country of miracles.

Everything ends as soon as it begins. Everything dies the moment it's born. Even the simplest things. Waking up in the morning. Going to market. Working the land. Giving birth to a boy or a girl. Everything is suddenly strange.

Par for the course are all the strange happenings called accidents of circumstance. A temporary interruption. A detour. A bump in the road. Water. Stones. Plains. Desert. Even anemones! Which ones are blessed and which are cursed? Nothing is simply water, stone, a plain, a desert, a flower, in this country of the miraculous.

— Only the naive believe in miracles. Me, I see what I have to see. I don't shift my gaze. It takes a clear-sighted seer to guide this gang of the blind. When they want miracles, I create some. With my fat fingers, I knit and unravel this country till it fits us like a glove — and for my trouble, my courage, they hate me. And you. You blind me. Paralyze me. Reduce me to a diseased and fetid corpse. Give them back! Give me back my eyes as you did my voice!

— I don't have them, Arik.

— Give me back my body!

— I don't have that, either.

— Give me back my life!

—I can't return something to you that was never yours. Life started before you and will end long after you do.

He hears water splashing. A damp silhouette brushes against him. Rita takes his hand in hers and places it on her breast.

—What are you doing?

Frightened, Arik withdraws his hand. Rita doesn't let it go.

—Touch me. I'm lending you my body.

He lightly grazes her moist body. Her feminine curves. Her face.

—Go on, inscribe my features in your memory. Provide me a face in the darkness. I'll be your mirror. Do you recognize me, Arik?

—No.

—Who were you before all the miracles? Who would we be were we ordinary people living in an ordinary country with other ordinary people—if we said to hell with miracles, to hell with promises? If we took pleasure in finding the same tree at the same crossroads, year after year?

Ordinary. The word sounds false in Arik's mouth. His face lights up. The word squirms on his tongue like a worm. Life drains from his face. Is this what it means to die? To have memory bleed out until nothing is left of him? Has he ever been ordinary?

The worm chews a hole in a drawer to which he

doesn't have the key. Must he die in order to find that key? He thinks of all the Palestinians who have languished in camps at the outskirts of the country for the past seventy years. Of the pathetic, rusted keys of their houses handed down from generation to generation. Unremarkable keys that nevertheless make a mockery of all his maps, roads, settlements. But not him. No. He's never been ordinary. The word is not a part of his lexicon.

He's a Jew, a Zionist, an Israeli. Child of a persecuted people. A Chosen People. A child of exile. Of ascension. Exceptional. The heir of an exceptional history.

Jew. Zionist. Israeli. Suffering is his cornerstone. He grew up naming the martyrs of the First Crusade from the *Memorbuchen*, the "memory books" of his father's library. The massacres of the first millennium fade into those of the second. The pogroms of the Russian Empire are inserted like so many other digressions in the accounts of the *Yizker bukh* and other remembrances of the Second World War.

Devastated lives.

The ruined dream of a Yiddish homeland.

Revived.

Lost again.

Revived again.

The names of martyrs recited for a thousand years.

Ritual after ritual.

Commemoration after commemoration.

Tragedy upon tragedy.

Jew. Zionist. Israeli. His own life is a tragedy. A scroll of the names of victims of bygone times and places uncoiling in no particular order. No time. No place. Its binding logic the cult of suffering. Unique, incomparable, exceptional suffering.

Jew. Zionist. Israeli. Destined to live apart from other peoples. Apart, even, from the rest of the Jews in the world. Most of all, those who want no part of the indivisible trinity, of being Jew, Zionist, Israeli. Who neither claim nor condemn Israel. Who aspire to no kind of liberation. Neither for themselves, nor the Palestinians. Sybarites who know nothing of suffering. Neither their own, nor that of the Palestinians. Who observe the suffering from a distance. Despair of it without lifting a halting finger.

Arik, at least, knows where the challenges lie. He learned to suffer even before confronting his own pain. Fought in the name of that suffering. History is the nail pricking him in the ass whenever he dares to sit down and enjoy a little happiness. How can he be ordinary when suffering is tattooed on his flesh?

In the beginning, he did not understand this. Why remain cautious and sad when he's happy? Why be wary of success? Why live as if defeat—or, worse, complacency—is always on the horizon? Why should every war won be nothing but a time bomb, an existential threat? As though each Israeli anniversary brings the country one year closer to its disappearance? Why, every Passover, did his parents and children say, do they say now, will they always say, "Next year in Jerusalem," when they've been eating, fucking, shitting, and sleeping in Jerusalem since 1967? Why, his entire life, since the day he was put on this land, for the duration of his growing up on this land, and until, no doubt, he dies on this land—if this woman ever does let him die—has he always been, is now, and forever will be, an exile?

He can't fathom it. But then his naivety gives way to cognition, his cognition to disenchantment, the disenchantment to cynicism, his cynicism to consciousness of the tarnished obligations of power. What had always seemed incomprehensible to him suddenly makes sense: without suffering, he would no longer know what it is to be a Jew, a Zionist, an Israeli.

His life. The arrival of his parents. His struggles. His battles. All the ignoble acts he ever committed—and he knows it, that certain of his acts have been ignoble— were undertaken in pursuit of the affirmation and renewal of this suffering. How to conceive of oneself as a Jew, a Zionist, an Israeli, otherwise? To divvy up the indivisible trinity of suffering, why would he do that when it carries so much weight?

Ordinary? No! He isn't, could *never* be, ordinary!

Now Palestinians are ordinary. They live simply. Take life as it comes. Live in the umbrage of their delights. Their sorrows. Their gains. Their losses.

Rooted, nothing and no one will ever tear them from the soil. The land acknowledges them, as they acknowledge the land. The land is always faithful to them.

Settlers. Pilgrims. Crusaders. They come. They go. Like the seasons. Temples are razed. Realms crumble. Caliphates. Even gods. But the peasants are there. Wake up every morning. Welcome the dawn. Work the land. Kiss the hooves of their horses before riding to the market. The merchants too, arriving at the souk in Old Jerusalem before the crowds do, each one sweeping the portion of the alley in front of their shop. Welcoming the villagers arriving for bread and provisions.

Someone must see to the daily business of living while believers prostrate themselves as they follow in the footsteps of Christ, or weep at the Western Wall. As tourists live out their fantasies of the Holy Land and the Orient. Someone needs to pick up after the enlightened. Water the orchards after the departure of the zealots, kings, and warriors.

The Palestinians remain, their presence as dependable as the beating of their hearts. A stubbornly ordinary people in a land infested with biblical legend. With miracles. With myths conjured behind the walls of castles a million miles away. Dreams harvested in the ghettos of foreign cities.

They'd come up against megalomaniac conquerors drunk on glory long before the *Nakbah* —because for Palestinians, the birth of Israel was well and truly a catastrophe—megalomaniacs easily dislodged by subsequent ones, their mania rapidly deflated by peasant life and its serene rhythms unaffected by the intemperate moods of emperors. But never had they faced such strength, omnipotence, tenacity. The invincibility of suffering. Its power of convocation. Invocation. Revocation. Its capacity to crush all resistance, from within or from without.

Its nimbleness.

A suffering that folds and unfolds time and place effortlessly. That manipulates the layers of history like an accordion. Draws sorrow from a bottomless well and dresses it in conviction.

And they were swept away, these stubborn, ordinary Palestinians.

Like so much dust on the surface of a sacred object.

—I've never been ordinary. I will never be ordinary. To be ordinary is a death sentence in this country.

—Let us die, then. Why not? Let's be ordinary together. We often are.

When I was young, I was beautiful. Ordinary. The earth danced under my feet when I skipped in the field. Horses neighed excitedly, their ears pricked up so they might hear my voice and fly in the wind.

—I loved horses too...

—I know that.

Rita pulls away from him. She gathers water in the palm of her hand and lets it run gently over Arik's white hair, massages his scalp. Repeats the gesture. On his face. His shoulders. His torso. Every limb.

—Come, Arik.

—Where to?

—Where it's still possible to be ordinary.

—Where's that?

—In the marketplace. Come quickly! The villagers are arriving with their horses. How do Arabians trot, Arik?

—As if they were the masters and the villagers their servants. Oh, I envy them...

—Who? The villagers or the horses.

—Both.

—Turn around. To the left. In that quiet corner of the market, do you see him?

—Who?

—A boy, standing apart while the other urchins clown around in front of the girls. He only has eyes for his mare.

—There's no boy.

—He's right there.

—I see nothing! You blinded me. Have you forgotten?

—Oh, Arik! There are other ways of seeing. Be strong. Look inside yourself.

An image rises up in him. The boy, obviously an Arab peasant boy, whispers softly to the mare. The white mare tilts her ears towards the boy's breathing.

Heaves a guttural sigh. It's familiar, this scene. His father, Shmuel, is at the market. So is he. They would have arrived together on their cart to buy provisions. Every week, the trip to the market was both exciting and terrifying. The 1930s, the Arab Revolt in full fury. The rebellion against the British, masters at the time, has degenerated into a General Strike. Outlaws like Abu Jilda, heroes to the peasants, are quickly executed by the Brits, soon to be replaced by other bandits risen from the revolutionary ranks: Izz ad-Din al-Qassam and his brigades. Al-Qassam! When he was a child, the name kept him from sleeping. Worse, the name would follow him throughout his life, stamped as it was on homemade rockets launched from the shantytowns and camps of Gaza. Sixty-nine years later, the name haunts him still.

Suddenly the boy turns towards Arik. You'd have thought the mare had slipped a word in the boy's ear about the stranger watching them. Has the boy noticed him? Are they laughing at him, the boy and his mare, sneering at his nakedness? His filth?

—Calm down, Arik. It's me they're looking at. The Jewish girl with golden tresses.

—What game are you playing at? This is not my story. Not my story!

—It's an alternative one. Did you not ask me who I was? It's another story of yours. Don't you want to know if there's another you breathing under this mass of flesh?

Rita scrubs the mounds and fissures of Arik's skin with a rough stone. She bathes him. The dirt on him dissolves and, with it, his shame. Rita's attentions become more insistent. Waves of good feeling shake him to his teeth.

—Listen, Arik. What do you hear?

He listens like he's never listened before. Behind the sounds of the marketplace he hears the sizzling of black, red, and yellow rocks under the sun's rays. The rustling of palm trees. The gurgling of oryx drinking at the edge of the spring. Farther off, from a grotto at the end of the desert, he hears Lily's voice mingling with the dewdrops. Forming stalactites. And even farther beyond, an echo behind the hills. The rounded sound of Arabic vowels linked like so many pearls. A necklace of words. A poem.

His breathing takes on the rhythm of Rita's caresses. His heart pounds behind his eyes, or is it the boy's Arab heart he hears?

—He has the gift of words.

—Who?

—The boy. He's reciting Arabic poems I don't understand. For two years, we were in love. At the marketplace, he would bring me fruit from his father's farm. He told me my name is the same in Arabic and Hebrew. That we shared the same heaven. Counted the same fluffy clouds, each from our own window. At night I'd wander about his village. We slept on straw, with his mare. In a little spot hidden away. No one existed but us and the horse. Then war broke out. Childhood deserted us. The boy no longer came to the marketplace. I no longer went to his village. No more horse between us. Only distance, and a million stories and poems.

—Where is he?

—He's here, in me. An almond blossom between my lungs. Smell it. Can you smell it, Arik?

He inhales. The smell of his desire. Odours emanating from his skin. Of perfume. A feminine fragrance left on his skin by her kisses. How he would love to let himself go, to dissolve into this woman-scent. To flee, to flee...

—Flight is impossible, Arik. All through the war I was unable to flee. If my parents called me, I hid in the barn.

Arik smiles despite himself. All those hours spent in the hayloft of his father's barn... He too, fleeing. The horses, agitated. He would rise and tend to them, soothe them with a carrot or...

—An apple.

The smell of fruit drifts from Rita's skin.

—Taste it, Arik.

He tastes Rita's body. Strange flavours tingling on his tongue. Seductive. Sweet. Bitter. Tastes of victory and defeat. Love. Hatred. Joy. Grief. Tastes of anger. Vengeance. Against the whole world. Tastes of anguish.

His own anguish at his failures. As a moshavnik. As a soldier. A politician.

Suddenly, he shivers. Is he still naked? He's almost forgotten. He presses himself against Rita. His withered body. His throat raw from incessant vomiting. He's thirsty. And so very hungry. Everything tastes good when you're hungry. The perfumed body of this woman. Her breasts heavy with milk.

A drop of milk in his mouth. Tepid. Forbidden. Mixed with the acrid tastes of gunpowder and tear gas. How many times has he heard it said, *The Arab suckles his hatred of Jews from his mother's breast*? Sentences whose only motive is to incite violence. And here he is, suckling!

What is he drinking? Hatred also? Love? Regret? Life? Death? Is she poisoning or curing him with her mother's milk? He drinks, and the desire to devour this creature mounts within him. Her voice. Her body flowing in and out of his, settling in his, separating from his. He is here. There. Man. Woman. Israeli. Palestinian. Predator. Prey. He loves. He detests. He no longer knows where he begins and where she ends. Whether theirs are two faces or one. Which face he wears. Which one she does.

He tears himself from her breast. Traces Rita's features with the tips of his fingers. Finds Vera's eyes. Lily's mouth. Gali's hair...And somewhere, between her breasts, Gour's heart. His cherished son buried amid the almond blossoms the little boy-poet planted there. It grows among the ruins. Spreads its perfume into Rita's lungs. But burns in him! Burns like a wound dressed with alcohol.

He sits up, his chest on fire.

—It burns, doesn't it? Run, run!

—Run where?

—As far as possible. We'll follow the setting sun.

—I can't see the sun.

—Then we'll follow the moon.

—I can't see the moon!

—Then we'll follow the stars.

He runs. Wearing Rita's body. Carried along by her lightness of being. The low murmur of her footsteps. The sand trembles. He is solid matter. Antimatter. A particle and its opposite. Something between what exists and what does not.

Is this what it is to be woman? To swim like a corpuscle in men's veins? To search for a soul at the bottom of this huge, sick body, and inject it with perfume that burns? To chastise men for their violence without ever being able to hate them? Why then, does she not hate him? He would hate himself if he were her. Wait: he *is* her! Fetus body and womb. Why has she let him inhabit her body like this? Is she not afraid he'll parasitize her? Or is she the parasite? Is she Death? Vengeance? Anguish?

—And if I were love, Arik?

He runs for hours and hours. Savours his emancipation from his own body, his obesity, his uselessness.
The burns of her perfume subside.

—Breathe, Arik.

He breathes.

A light kiss on his left eyelid. A point of light. Faint,
at first, it gently illuminates the darkness. A kiss on his
right eyelid. Light haloes the black.

—Open your eyes, Arik.

The night brightens.

He sees. Sees! He feels the skin that envelops him.
At his touch, it changes. Disintegrates. Reassembles
just beyond his reach. Is she a ghost? A phantom? He
scrutinizes his surroundings. The source. He's still at
the source. But has he not been running for hours? Has
he been going in circles? Is there no end to this fluid
mass that follows him wherever he goes?

The sound of distant galloping. The Arab boy's
mare. She is suspended in the meadow. Wild and free.
Cuts through the half-light. Her skin glows like satin.
Her mane licks the wind. She gallops. Unbridled.
Sleek. Cresting the waves of wheat. Clearing a Milky
Way.

The horse enters a village on the horizon. Is it a
horizon or border? What border? No checkpoint, no
soldiers. Simply a feeling. A limit. An invisible line. And
if he crossed that line?

—Cross it, Arik.

A young man appears on the horizon. Arik recognizes him immediately. It's the boy from the market. He's grown. He joins the mare, murmurs something in her ear, rubs her neck. She's still the same. Hasn't aged. Is eternal. Suddenly he bows down and kisses the right hoof of the mare, then her left.

Until this moment, Arik has never realized a human could love an animal so much. He thought he alone knew how to love horses. He thought he'd passed this love on uniquely to Gour. And that this love died with Gour. But this Arab's love preceded his! Is there nothing he possesses that wasn't first owned by peasants?

Like two lovers, the man and horse disappear over the horizon.

—Arik, Arik...

—Leave me alone.

—They're here.

The earth trembles. Shadows rush towards him, wearing the colours of the Israeli army. He signals to them. The soldiers reach him. No one looks him in the eye. They pass him by. Turn towards the village. Bullets fly. Ricochet off the rocks. Fill the sky with flashes of light. The soldiers lay siege to the village, awaiting further orders. Further orders are slow in coming. Silence descends. And boredom.

War is boring. A series of long waits and morbid weariness, war is.

Wait for GO! For the next push.

Wait for GO! For the next death.

Wait for GO! For the next hail of bombs.

Hold your fire for the ceasefire.

Arik has a pretty good idea about all this, he who is always more bored than anyone else.

Terrible company, boredom is, when you're twenty and have a gun in your hand. Camped around the village, the soldiers wait. Some of them are smart enough to sleep. Others play cards. But some of them feel a tingling in their ears. On the backs of their necks. Down their arms. A terrible tingling that stirs the sauce of impatience, fear, lightness in the chest. That explodes in savage sores. That demands to be scratched. Until you draw blood.

Suddenly, one of the scouts sees a shepherd. At last, a distraction! A wink to his comrades. A burst of fire from his machine gun. The sheep run off, terrified.

The shepherd's distress.

The soldiers' laughter.

Then...silence. More waiting. More boredom. Is there no respite from this ennui?

Which is when the white mare appears. She crosses the field, lowers her beautiful mane. Grazes calmly. One of the soldiers leaves his unit. His skin is itching so badly he's unable to sit still. He needs to shoot. If he doesn't fire, the itches will kill him. He fixes the sight of his weapon on the glossy animal. Yes. Die. Die! Blood must run. He can't stand the boredom any longer, the sores proliferating everywhere on his body.

He shoots with the frenzy of fingernails scratching at an insect bite.

He shoots like he's scraping. Like he's sanding. Like he's peeling.

When the mare goes down, he breaks into insane laughter.

The man who kissed the mare rushes to her side. Other soldiers rise to their feet. Which of them will shoot the peasant? One, a little wilier than the others, finds a good perch, lies flat on his stomach, his rifle braced in his forearms.

A bullet whistles.

The man's silhouette crumbles. And all his poems crumble.

A terrible cry bursts from the village. Shots striate the sky. The soldiers, emboldened by their comrades, advance through the fields. Riddle the windows of the village houses with bullets. Crush the fruit and vegetables underfoot. Beat the villagers who rush to save the orchards. Other soldiers gather in the centre of the village and count the goats drowned in blood.

— Boredom is the most murderous of feelings. How many have been killed, Arik, to appease the pent-up idleness of fevered men?

— Shut up.

— The orders will come eventually. The soldiers

will empty the village as you would a pantry before cleaning it out.

—Stop.

—Slowly. Methodically.

—No!

—The men will be herded. The subjected chained. The resisters neutralized.

—Not another word!

—The women, children, and the aged loaded into trucks.

—Are you trying to kill me?

—No, Arik. I killed once and for all.

—Leave me alone, witch!

—Don't you wish to know who I am anymore? My story doesn't end here.

—Where, then?

Here he is in the barn of his childhood. It's as though he's seeing the horses of the moshav for the first time. Their abused bodies. Worn teeth. Heads lowered, tethered to the walls of their stalls. Their defeated looks speak to him: You are no more free, nor the master of your destiny, than we are, they say. Imbecile! You'll die in that grotesque body of yours. Your skin in tatters. Your face drained.

—No! No! No! It's not here that everything ends!

—No... it's here that everything begins.

A torch flies into the barn. Flames ignite in the straw. Lick the walls.

—Who threw that torch? Who?

Arik dashes into the barn. Gour will never forgive him if he lets the horses die. He opens the stalls. Unties the animals.

—Run! Run! Save yourselves!

The horses remain, stunned, as flames form an infernal circle around them. Arik whips them.

—Save yourselves, you stupid animals!

—Arik... Arik...

—No!

—It's too late. The horses have been dead a long time.

—Why? Was it for revenge?

—For freedom.

I, too, was twenty years old when they wanted to make an assassin of me. But I killed death instead. Once. Twice. A thousand times. Fire devoured the horses in the barn and devoured me with them. May 14, 1948, it was. The day the poet in me died was the day the country was born. The day my country was born, I killed myself.

Since then, I die and am reborn. I am the woman-nightingale. The woman-voice. I criss-cross the country. Its hills. Valleys. Deserts. Lakes. Rivers. I paw and trample the earth. My only rider is the fury of women. Their dreams. Desires. Nightmares. I killed the horses and committed suicide.

—Traitor!

—Rita. I am Rita. It was the poet who gave me that name.

I am born the day of my death. A stillborn child, in a stillborn country. I dress myself up in the lives of others. I roam the Earth. Float through the sky. I gather souls. Carry them on my back and on my wings. Every time my wings catch fire, I kill myself and rise again, reborn, from my ashes. Deep lines are chiselled in my face. One for each life. One day I'll be nothing but lines etched on the face of death. Stories erased. Destinies beaten into the cheeks of this land. On that day, I will at last be no one. Do you recognize me now?

—Who are you?

—Her.

A female soldier stands apart from her comrades. They are brutalizing the village and its inhabitants. She refrains from joining them. Turns and looks at the devastation.

—And her.

A young girl in the settlement searches for her balloon. It's floating over an empty soccer field. Beneath the artificial turf, a mass grave.

—And her.

An adolescent woman in uniform moves towards the surveillance tower to take her shift by the wall. Today's task: shove women and children in the back.

Voices.

—Where are the voices coming from?

—From the source. They are the echo of all the arrested beginnings. All the voices in me. Every time I die, I return to the source.

—What source?

—The source that leads to another end.

—Are you my end?

—I am the beginning and the end. Did Vera not tell you?

—Are you my mother?

—I am your mother and the woman your mother was never able to be. In one of my lives, the Arabs called me the Gazelle; the Jews called me the Eccentric. I cared for victims and their murderers. Jews and Arabs. Once, I sewed up the wounded chin of a boy who'd fallen off his donkey. His mother had travelled for kilometres rather than take him to the clinic in their moshav. Her name was Vera. Her son, Ariel.

—It's you? Still you! How long have you been haunting me? Give me back my mother! Give me back my Gali! Give me back my Lily! Give me back my life, you stealer of lives!

—I am her, and her, and her —

Golda, the iron woman. Hannah, the woman of light. Rita. Poem. Voice. I am. Warrior. Philosopher. Woman-of-war. The one who reads books to you as you lie on your deathbed. I am all the beautiful and perverse lives birthed by this country. I am the raptor and the sweetly singing nightingale. The white mare, the black mare. To come to terms with death, I've mastered the spirits of men.

Say nothing more, Arik. I understand the secret language of eyes. I have solved the mystery of faces. The torment in your gaze. You. Vera. Lily. Gali. Every crease. Every altered dimple. The drooped eyelids. The lips split by wounds. The breathing suppressing rage. Don't hide the stench, Arik. I can detect the odour of hearts. Clothe myself—like a silkworm—in the waves that saturate space. Discern the wretch hanging out with innocents.

In all my lives and deaths, I let myself be devoured. Bitten. Chewed. Sucked into the bowels of snakes. I've squeezed my body against my soul. Drunk the semen of toads. Nursed murderers of children. Made rapists cry out in their ecstasy. From my animal-woman body I have forged a blade to skin the monsters who think themselves men.

—I am not a monster. I am human. Enough suffering. Enough death! What good is war if there can be no taste of victory? Is it so terrible to always want more? To always be hungry? Why settle for a mouthful when we can lick the plate? Why limit ourselves to a full belly when we can gorge on everything? Why tighten our belts when we can spread out like water on a smooth surface? All my life I've been told to suffer, to restrain my gluttony. Why deprive myself of so much pleasure?

—Is it pleasure you want, Arik?

Suddenly, the sound of a body plunging into water. The water he thought he'd left behind long ago. Water that follows him, nibbles at his ankles. Water infested with tentacles desperate to strangle him. Water that erases him entirely whenever he tries to free himself of it. He's tired. Tired of fighting the current. The water is warm. Irresistibly warm. He wants nothing more than to sink into its warmth.

—Let the tide carry you away, Arik. Carry away everything that clings to your skin. Everything you've vomited. Everything you've swallowed. The toxic pelts eating away at you. And if I wiped away all the layers of your body? Your memory? What would be left of you, Arik?

A hand between his legs. She spreads them apart. He resists.

She bathes the insides of his thighs. Massages the folds of surplus skin.

—What if I freed you from your pleasures? What would be left of you, Arik?

She caresses him. Rinses him. Caresses him. Rinses him. His desire increases. His pudgy toes flex. His wasted muscles stiffen under the pull of his heavy skin. His drooping breasts harden.

—What are you doing? What are you doing? Stop!

—Giving you the pleasure you desire.

She cups her palms between his legs. Nothing exists

now except the rise and fall of her hands. The squeezing that pulls and releases. Squeezes. Pulls. Releases. Squeezes. Pulls. Releases. The tempo increases. The friction burns.

Suddenly, a warmth. His rigid member. His veins filled with blood. His whole body is covered in the caramel warmth of hot milk. Steaming milk.

Arik tries to free himself. Full lips close around his member. Coat it with saliva. Rob him of the little control he has left. Lead him towards the place where his fantasies run wild. His passions. His irruptions. To where his impulses boil. The temptation to drive a bulldozer over all who loathe him. Judge him. Block him. Even his friends! To the place where resentments and old grudges mix. Where the beast withdraws to suck marrow from the bones of its prey. The place he thought forever buried in his fat. The woman is twisting him with her lips. Without mercy. Twisting. Wringing him out. Drop after drop.

The night turns to indigo. Indigo turns purple. Purple to red. Red to orange. Orange to yellow. Yellow to white. A blinding white. A pitiless white. White on white on white!

He's going to come. She'll swallow all his strength. She'll take everything. Strip him of power. Rob him of everything. Everything that is him. Everything he has built!

—Vera! Where are you! Save me, Vera!

The terror mixes with pleasure. Terror before the secret wish that has inhabited him from childhood. The wish to free himself of the beast. That someone would open him up and deliver it from him. Once and for all. But no, not yet. Not right now. There's nothing in him but the beast. Nothing!

—Then be nothing, Arik. Is that such a bad thing? To be nothing and start afresh?

—Gali! Gali! She's devouring me.

—Be nothing, Arik. You'll never be hungry again.

—Lily! Get me out of here. I'm begging you. My Lily!

—Come, Arik. Come!

—Lily! Lily!

—Come!

—Lily!

His cry shreds the whiteness. Silhouettes shimmer in the light, just beyond his reach. They're all there! Uri, Gilad, Inbal. His grandchildren. They've grown! What sad faces. The women are there, too: Vera, Lily, Gali. Their translucent figures.

His vertebrae tremble. His bones crack. He feels them. His veins, burning. The electric shock of the spasm rushing through his devastated body. He hears them. The poundings of his heart beating one on top of the next until they are a single noise. Strident. Incessant. An endless note.

He bellows.

Loud.
Louder.
Louder still!
His orgasm is so ferocious he blacks out.

ARIK

—Tell me the truth, doctor. How long does he have?

Lips pinched, the doctor gestures for Gilad and Inbal to sit down. They sit across from him, in the same synthetic leather chairs in which they've so often heard news, both good and bad, about the state of Arik's health.

—It's a matter of hours...

Gilad turns pale. Inbal, with a pained expression, takes her husband's hand, as much to comfort him as to keep herself from collapsing. Gilad stares at the digital calendar on the corner of the doctor's desk. The screen says January 11, 2014. Eight years, almost to the day, since Arik went into a coma. *Aba*. He's frozen in place, hypnotized by the date. The only indication of shock is his fingers clenching those of his wife. The cold numbers of the clock hammer away at him, marking, without a familiar tick-tock, the passage of time.

The countdown has begun. It actually started a long time ago, but Gilad refused to believe it. His father has been suffering from a persistent urinary infection for a few months already, one of the perverse side effects of the continued use of a catheter to drain the bladder.

— It often occurs with people his age, explains the doctor. Wear and tear on the body is part of the natural order of things, even in the comatose.

Strange. The notion of Arik continuing to age reassures Gilad. Yet another proof that his father is alive, that he's present, that he belongs to the same world as him. But now the infection is causing renal failure. His organs are giving up one by one. Death is quietly sneaking up on him, consuming his body from within.

— We should tell the family, Gilad murmurs to his wife after a long silence.

Inbal nods in agreement. She takes out her cellphone. Whispers a few words — to family members, to friends. A final call to the children. Before leaving the doctor's office, she kisses her husband on the forehead.

— Don't be long…

— I'll be back with the children as soon as possible. And she's gone.

— Will he suffer, doctor? asks Gilad. Is he suffering now?

— Death is not necessarily painful. And is less and less so now, thanks to advances in palliative care. In certain cases, like that of your father, after such a long wait death can be…a relief. Well, a liberation, if you will.

Gilad returns to his father's room. She's there. As she always is. At his bedside, a book in hand. The Nightingale. Of all the hospital staff, she's the one who knows Arik the most intimately. She bathes him once a week. Cuts his hair and nails. And even though a physiotherapist visits him regularly, it's the Nightingale who massages his arms and legs, all the while whispering things to him that Gilad never quite manages to hear. If his mother were still alive, she'd be green with jealousy.

He's often surprised the nurse in conversation with his father, responding to questions no one but she could hear. Once Gilad asked her how she knew what ran through the head of a man in a coma. She simply caressed Arik's cheek and said:

—He speaks to me through his body, his face, his eyes.

—Does he recognize you?

—He sees other women in me. Women he knew. He recognizes the stories I tell him.

She's certainly told him many stories, thinks Gilad as he contemplates the books burgeoning around his bed. On this day—on what might well be the last day of his life—he lies soothed by the voice of this woman reading to him as she has done every day for years. Sometimes, she recites poems to him. Other times, she reads him novels in Hebrew, in Russian, in Hungarian, in French, in German, even in Arabic. It's astonishing to think that this woman has kept her secrets from him for eight years.

The Nightingale reading to his father is one of the scenes he'll miss when... Such insignificant routines come to pass in the most dramatic situations. For all those who gravitate around Arik, the regular beat of the heart monitor has marked time for eight years. The slow ticking away of seconds, minutes, days. How will they keep track of time when Arik is dead? Gilad has been measuring his weeks, his months, his years, by Arik's breathing.

The nurse looks up at him as though she has read his thoughts.

—Here.

She passes him the book, open to the page she's been reading.

—Khaled, the rebel, kisses the right hoof of Hamama, his mare. Then the left. Together, they disappear over the horizon. Naked. Free. The two of them are one. I must have read this story to Arik a thousand times, and still he wants to hear it again. And again...

Gilad hesitates.

—He must like hearing it in your voice.

Gilad takes the novel in his hands. Its title is *Time of White Horses*. The author: Ibrahim Nasrallah. The language, Arabic.

Gilad abruptly puts the book down.

—No! Arabic will not be the last language he hears.

—Arabic is in him, as it is in you.

—Who are you to tell me what's a part of me!

She smiles.

Palestinian Quebecker YARA EL-GHADBAN is an anthropologist by training but has been writing since she was thirteen. She is the author of three novels, of which *I Am Ariel Sharon* is the first to be translated into English. In 2017 she won the Canada Council for the Arts' Victor Martyn Lynch-Staunton Award, and in 2019 she was awarded the Blue Metropolis Literary Diversity Prize. She lives and writes in Montreal.

WAYNE GRADY is an award-winning author, translator, and editor. He has won the John Glassco Translation Prize and the Governor General's Literary Award for Translation and was a finalist for the Governor General's Literary Award two additional times. His debut novel, *Emancipation Day*, won the Amazon.ca First Novel Award. He lives near Kingston, Ontario, with his wife, novelist Merilyn Simonds.